Bedtime Stories
from the
Outer Banks

Bedtime Stories

from the
Outer Banks

WALT JOHNSON

iUniverse, Inc.
Bloomington

Bedtime Stories from the Outer Banks

iUniverse books may be ordered through booksellers or by contacting:

iUniverse
1663 Liberty Drive
Bloomington, IN 47403
www.iuniverse.com
1-800-Authors (1-800-288-4677)

ISBN: 978-1-4759-6186-7 (sc)
ISBN: 978-1-4759-6187-4 (ebk)

Printed in the United States of America

iUniverse rev. date: 01/21/2013

Please read for safety's sake before reading the book:
(It's *REALLY* short)
There are several situations in these stories that need first aid or quick thinking. This is not a first aid manual. Seek professional advice for that. The Mayo Clinic has excellent first aid sites. Also, when starting surfing it is a good idea to sign up with a surf school and start on a soft surfboard. As a past lifeguard and having a brother who had four teeth knocked out while learning surfing, I thought I should mention that. There. Now I can sleep at night.

Walt

PS. Visit my Facebook page, Bedtime Stories from the Outer Banks, if you like the book and leave me a message. I would really like to hear from you.

Chapter 1

"So, have you ever been in love?" asked Jean.

There was a quart of vodka on the table and Jean, pronounced more like zchon (a blend of Shawn and John), as he was French, was about to take a shot. Tom bought the bottle because Jean had just had some bad luck with a girl he was dating. It was a strange question coming from Jean whose motto was "Never fall in love, it is *ze* end to all *appiness.*"

"I loved Patricia," replied Tom

"*Thees* is not what I asked."

Tom got edgy and scoffed. "I know."

Tom just let his mind drift back to exactly where he knew it would go. "Once, I'm pretty sure. And you know, what really pisses me off is that I didn't even date her that long. Not even that consistently. I dated Pat for four years, but I never had that 'in love' feeling. I was never in love with her the way I was with Sue."

He then thought back to her green eyes, slender figure, and long blonde hair. It was all too hokey, and it drove him nuts. But there was that feeling, that damn feeling he almost despised.

"Yeah, I guess I was in love once: with a girl I hardly knew. And it was probably just because she was beautiful. And that, my friend, is how screwed up love is: or I am."

Jean thought for a moment and then leaned back and laughed a laugh that always lifted Tom's spirits. "Don't worry Tom, I know how you feel."

Tom looked at him glad to have some reassurance. Because Tom thought it was *very* screwed up, these feelings that had little justification as far as he was concerned.

"Do you now??" asked Tom. "Then how bout enlightening me. Because I *don't* know how I feel."

"Of course," replied Jean. "*Et es* not you. *Et's* love. *Et's* a very screwed up thing. *Louk* at me, I am *meserable*, and I was not even in love, thanks God! Imagine if I was?! Ah! *Ze* damn love! Sometimes, I think ze French are insane! At least in America you can like *szombody.* Do you know, in France, there is no word for like? Merde! There *es* only *ze* verb aimer, which means 'to love' or 'to like' depending on how you say it. One *sleep* and you are screwed! You say it *ze* wrong way and you end up in love. You see *ze* trap? You are screwed in France!

"I will never go back to France again! *Des* way, I will never have to be in love again. I will just like *evreeybody!* I will be a happy guy! Now pass *ze* bottle," requested Jean as he held out his hand.

"So what do you want to do tonight?" asked Tom.

"We chase *ze* girls, of course," replied Jean.

"I thought you were sick of love," said Tom.

"I am, but *ze* girls, *zey* are in my nature. Who am I to fight all nature?

Chapter 2

And now, one year later, he was standing at the airport waiting to meet her. He hadn't seen her in ten years. On a lark he sent her a mailing catalog from his business. She had called him back. She was curious, and lonely. At this point she didn't mind the risk. Her marriage had ended badly, as only one can, and he had crossed her mind. She remembered how they had kept up over the years, but had lost touch after her marriage. When she got the catalog in the mail, she smiled inwardly. A smile she had forgotten she was capable of.

She called and the conversation went well. Right away she felt easy and comfortable and had not done something she had not done in some time: laughed. And before it was over, they decided she should come down for a visit. It was summer; he lived on the beach. Not the same beach where they had met in New Jersey, another in North Carolina. Tom sensed she could use a change of scenery and suggested she come down for a little relaxation. Her heart made a funny little leap. At the end of the conversation, they made plans for her to come down in three weeks.

He couldn't meet her at the gate because of security so he waited in the terminal. He remembered back to when they were younger how he used to meet her at the kite store where she worked. How he awoke with her in her little apartment on the beach. He still remembered the song that was playing on the radio when he awoke, and it reminded him of her every time he had heard it since. He was annoyed he was nervous. Tom controlled things, and this included his emotions. He was no longer in love with her, of course. Just because he was once in love with her, or whatever that was, it did not mean he had to stay that way. He once thought one of his best qualities was the ability to walk away from a bad relationship and leave it quickly. He would not let anyone or anything control him. He left his teaching job for a little business for just that reason. Too much politics. He did not make a great amount of money in his store yet, but he called the shots. He called the shots in business, and he called the shots with his emotions.

He paced a bit. And suddenly, there she was, much the same. She was still beautiful and slender, and that wasn't helping matters. Her hair was long as he had remembered: a mix of auburn and blonde. Her smile was intelligent and peculiar, as only a smile can be when meeting a lover whom one has not seen in a long time.

"Hey," she said brightly as she walked up to him and stopped just a foot or two short from where he was standing.

"Sue Coburn," he said, "as he eyed her up and down. "Why you just look . . . terrible," he said flatly, his smile painting over the lie.

"I look better than YOU!" she parried.

"Oh, shut up. I was always cuter than you, and you know it."

"Yeah right," she scoffed sarcastically. "You were always a bigger jackass. I remember that."

She stood looking at him with a half cocked smile.

"So," she said.

"So what?" he replied.

She then kicked him in the shins.

"I flew four hundred miles to see your sorry ass. You could at least give me a hug or something!"

He rolled his eyes as if it were an effort and moved deliberately toward her. He slipped his arm around her waist and was a bit frightened at the familiar feeling that surrounded his heart.

He warned her over the phone the business was new and not yet making much money. He had moved into the back of the store to keep expenses low. It was actually a large storeroom he fixed into a little apartment. It was small, but clean and well organized, air conditioned and cool, and had a bathroom and a shower. It was comfortable; and it was his.

Upon entering the store she was immediately enchanted. It was full of jewelry, which was in good taste, she noted, in the atmosphere of a rainforest. Little mechanical monkeys and birds hung from the vines on the rafters and chattered and sung softly through the African music played through the store. When you stepped into the store, you felt like you entered another world. The effect Tom wanted.

"It's wonderful," Sue said. She meandered around and looked at the jewelry and other items in the store. She held up a pair of earrings she fancied and turned toward Tom with a smile.

"Don't get any ideas. This is a business."

She made a face as she cuddled the earrings before her.

She doesn't have to be so damn cute and funny! Tom thought as he laughed at her.

"That's the only pair for you," he said.

Her smile broke beautifully. She smiled for two reasons. She had her earrings and she had gotten her way. She walked up to Tom and hugged him. "Now that wasn't so bad, was it?"

"What wasn't?"

"Giving in."

"I didn't give in to anything. I want you to have them."

She stood and stamped her feet a little.

"You gave in and you know it!"

"Oh think what you want," he smiled.

They went to the back of the store to the room Tom had fixed into an apartment. "It's small, I warned you."

As they walked in, Tom got defensive. He knew Sue's dad was loaded and most of her friends were. "It's a rat hole. Go on and say it. This is your chance to live it up."

"It's okay," she said. "It's free, it's clean, and the company MIGHT be acceptable."

"There's no TV," she said. "How do you entertain yourself?"

"Read, play guitar, write."

"Write?"

"Sure."

"Write what?"

"Grocery lists."

She walked over to the shelves with manila folders on them. She ran her fingers along them.

"They are stories?"

"You are a regular Sherlock Holmes, you are."

"Can I hear one?"

"If you want to have some fun, you can have all the fun you want by insulting my little castle by the sea here; I see no reason to let you be able to make fun of my writing next."

She made a face.

"C'mon, we'll go get some dinner," said Tom, and he let the subject drop.

Chapter 3

Arriving late at the store things got awkward. They walked into the little room in the back.

"You can sleep here. I have a sleeping bag and will stay in the store. I mean, I didn't invite you here with any expectations."

Sue expected this. Tom liked control. But over himself and his world. Not over people. He was never pushy toward anyone.

"Oh don't worry about it. It's a double bed. We can share. I don't want to kick you out of your own bed for crying out loud."

Tom got ready first. He took enough time brushing his teeth and washing his face so she would have time to change. When he came out, she was in a T-shirt and a pair of shorts. As she was in the bathroom, he changed into some shorts and slipped into bed. The quilts and sheets were freshly washed and felt clean as sunshine all around him. He chuckled at how much he appreciated little things like that.

As she returned from the bathroom, she shook her hair from her face. She slid her shorts off over her panties and climbed into bed. She smelled even fresher than the sheets.

She smacked him on the ass and felt his shorts.

"Just checking."

"Don't flatter yourself"

She leaned back and put her arms under her head.

"Okay now, I'm ready."

"Ready for what?"

"My bedtime story is what!"

"I thought you forgot about that."

"No, really," she said sincerely, "I want to hear one."

"I don't know."

There was something inside her that knew she would enjoy the story.

"Okay, I can see I have to earn this one." She made a flirtatious face and fluttered her eyelashes. "Please," she whimpered.

Tom was amused, and it relaxed him.

"Okay, princess, I'll read you a story."

He got up and pulled one from the shelf.

"But if you laugh, you sleep on the beach."

When he came back to the bed, he did not slip right in. He crossed over her.

"My side," he said.

"I remember," she replied. He had always slept to the left of her, her head nestled over his arm resting on his chest. She was just lying next to him now, however, letting herself enjoy her little memory.

"This one is called, 'The Telescope Man.'"

He then began to read. His voice poured smoothly into the pool of light that shone on the story. She was happy and safe. And if she ever had a problem in her life, she could not remember it now.

"Spinning around in the Milky Way somewhere, there was a dark volcanic eye peering out at the universe," Tom said as he began the story. "It was at the end of a long telescope in Nags Head, North Carolina: a barrier island which was once inhabited by Blackbeard, and where the Wright brother's first flew using a machine to propel them. The eye belonged to Mark Scharf, who owned the shop called The Telescope Store. But to all the kids that packed the store every night, he was known as 'The Telescope Man.'"

Tom glanced over at Sue and felt more comfortable to see she was relaxed and enjoying herself. She met his eyes and smiled. She could not help herself from what she did next. She pulled Tom's right arm down and nestled it around her neck and put her head on his chest.

So this is happiness, she thought.

She looked up at Tom for assurance and he smiled down to her.

"Go ahead," she murmured.

Chapter 4

The Telescope Man

Three times Abigail passed by the telescope store. She stared wide eyed as she watched the man in the telescope store show different kids the craters in the moon, stars in the sky, and distant planets in the heavens. The store was like another world. Pictures of the galaxy, stars, and planets illuminated the midnight blue walls of the shop. As you looked into the store, you couldn't help feel bigger, or perhaps more knowledgeable about the world. You were no longer just a being on earth; it was no longer your home. The universe was your new home, here, in the telescope store.

Three times she passed it getting up the nerve to enter the universe. As usual, there was a crowd of kids gathered around a magnificent telescope mounted in the window of the store and pointed toward the heavens. The telescope man then let the next small boy peer through the scope.

"What do you see there?" asked the telescope man.

"The biggest star in the sky," replied the boy in wonder.

"One would think so," said the telescope man, "but actually, it is a planet. It's Venus. Everything is different in space. Sometimes what you see as a very dim star is actually brighter than a thousand suns. And there, where you see a bright star, there is really no light being given off. It is just reflected light. Like Venus there. Everything is different in space. Proportion, time, space, all these things become so relative you can hardly believe your own eyes any longer."

"It's awesome," sighed the boy.

"And for all we know someone is looking at us. They may have flown from another galaxy to explore, much the same Columbus did on this planet, but their world is the universe. They are not baffled that it goes on forever; they are grateful. Because in forever there is always another adventure. They hover about in the night, quietly without lights on and travel in stealth. They veer in and veer out quickly so not to be noticed as they keep an eye on this little blue ball and listen in to our conversations. We confuse them. They see we have enough technology and resources to have a paradise here: but we don't. They see us work and work when it is not even necessary to do so any longer instead of enjoying this planet. They see arguments and violence, and people not sharing the wealth of the planet. Our race confounds them. They would land, but surely these earthlings who can't even get along with one another may not get along with them. So they wait under the cover of darkness and silence and watch. Watch and wait for us to discover how wonderful life can be."

"What a bunch of bullshit!" shouted a smart aleck teenager from the back of the crowd by the door. The telescope man rose and stood high. He was six foot three, slim with broad shoulders and an athletic build. His eyes were brown and volcanic. His hair black as the night. He turned slowly to the boy and gazed at him with new emotion. The kid swallowed a little. He had no idea what the telescope man looked like when he was sitting on the stool. He figured he was just some nerd to play with. Tall, mysterious, and consuming the telescope man called to the boy.

"Come over here, young man."

The boy was losing his composure now. He expected the telescope man to be embarrassed and to bow to the will of the boy. The kid thought he would have fun and prove himself a big man by mocking out this nerdy star gazer. But it was plain to see the telescope man could make short work of him and all his friends if he wanted to.

"Prove to me I am wrong. Without a shadow of a doubt. And be prepared for a good argument. I know a little of the universe and its possibilities. We have sent probes to Mars. You don't think someone else may be out there with better technology? Really? I am not saying they have. I am saying it is a possibility. Don't be so consumed with your knowledge, or the knowledge of all of man's history for that matter. Einstein was much more enamored by human imagination than the knowledge we have acquired."

The boy then gazed around the store at the charts the man knew so well. He was sure the telescope man knew the climate of every planet in this solar system and more. Books everywhere: about the moon, planets, solar systems, space travel, and the boy was sure the telescope man had read them all.

"Well?" said the telescope man.

But the boy was not about to be out staged by an adult.

"Oh, give me a break with all this. Anyone can imagine anything."

"Can they?" The telescope man pondered the question seriously. He had never really had this thought before. He learned a little something from this boy tonight.

The telescope man saw the boy sneaking interested gazes at the telescope. The telescope man swung the telescope to the moon.

"Why not have a look?"

The boy peered into the scope and was struck speechless as he gazed at the surface of the moon. It was as if the telescope pulled him out through the window and into space. The telescope man then began to tell the boy the names of the different craters and mountain ranges on the moon as the boy swung the telescope to and fro to gaze upon this little satellite of earth. After a minute or two the teenager pulled away. As he looked around the store, he felt as if he did not belong there. He belonged on the moon.

"What do you think?"

The boy, realizing the telescope man was not looking for an argument, became civil.

"It was . . . great. A great telescope."

"For a great lad, eh?"

The boy smiled. He chatted with the telescope man for a while under the watchful eye of Abigail. She stood still in the door. As the telescope man breathed, she breathed. Surely there was magic in this man. She was spellbound by his features. Dark and sharp, but smooth somehow. It seemed everyone walked out of The Telescope Store a little different than when they walked in. Abigail liked the telescope man the way all the other kids did. When you were in his shop, kids felt like adults and adults felt like kids. You felt special to be handed these great secrets of the universe. And when you walked home through the parking lot, you owned all the stars and promised to keep all their secrets.

Abigail was no exception. She stood by the car glaring at the stars as her mother fumbled around in her pocketbook for her keys. "Darn," said her mother. But when she looked up from her purse, Abby was gone.

"Abby!" screamed her mother. "Abigail!" Her mother's biggest fear is that she would run to the ocean, so she crossed the dune as she called and called.

But Abigail was running in the opposite direction. Up along the side of the water fall, past the toy store, the jewelry store, and finally, to the telescope store.

She peeped around the corner and saw the telescope man peering through the big telescope in the window. Stern and hard like the captain of a ship looking for land, he stared through the scope. Surely this man had all the answers, she thought. She slowly put one foot in front of the other and crept into the store. She was cute as they come. Blonde shoulder length hair, round blue eyes, that little girl complexion bonded together with what only little girls care for better than anyone: innocence. But with innocence comes shyness. She was timid and had the look of a squirrel when you get too close to one.

The telescope man sensed her presence and turned toward her.

"Hello," said the telescope man. His voice deep and reassuring as the ocean.

"Hey," whispered Abigail.

"Can I help you?"

"My mom said I could come up and get a look through the telescope," she lied. "It was too busy before."

"Sure," he said, "come on over."

Abigail peered through the scope, and it was surely magical. Her eyes sped along at the speed of light as her soul hung tightly on for the ride. She was going so fast she was dizzy.

"Like the view?"

"Oh, yes," she replied, "it is just as I thought it would be!" She hung tight to the scope and swung it to and fro. She did not seem to be simply looking at the stars. She was searching, searching for something. Her hand grasped the scope hard and she peered through the lens with an intensity the telescope man had never seen before.

"What are you looking for? Perhaps I can help you find it."

"Heaven," said Abigail, still staring through the scope.

"Heaven?" asked the telescope man.

"Yes," said Abigail. "My sister is there."

"I see," said the telescope man hiding the sadness in his voice.

Abigail then turned the lens away from her eye and stared into the volcanic glass of the telescope man's eyes.

"Mister," she said, "can you show me where heaven is so I can see my sister. My mom says she is up there, and safe. But." Her eyes then filled with some tiny tears and she continued as bravely as she could. "If only I could be sure. If I could be sure maybe, I wouldn't cry so at night." The tears then welled up and flowed down her cheek. And the next request was spoken like a prayer, "Please say you can do it sir."

The telescope man looked at her long and hard. He brushed the blond hair away from her cheek and placed his fingers under her chin and lifted her face up until it met his. It came out of his mouth before he could stop it. "Yes, you can see her through the telescope."

"Abigail!" screeched her mother. "Where have you been?! I have been looking all over for you. Oh Abigail, this is just like your dreamy little self to wander off like this. I thought we discussed this? Do you ever spend more than five minutes with both feet on the ground?"

"But Mom!" shouted Abigail with glee, "The telescope man said . . ."

"Now Abigail," interrupted the telescope man, "what you saw and heard tonight must remain a secret. Like wishing on a falling star." The telescope man then looked up at Abigail's mother and winked as he told Abigail, "You must not tell your wish, or it will not come true."

Abigail's mother pulled Abigail toward her. "I'm sorry she bothered you."

"No bother at all."

Abigail and her mother then disappeared as so many things do. The telescope man then turned gravely toward his scope as he slowly ran his hand along the barrel of the scope. "Jesus," he whispered.

The next evening the telescope man was working the crowd as usual. The cash register sang along as he sold glowing stars, little telescopes, maps to the galaxies, books about the moon, and extraterrestrial visitors. The lights were now off in the store and there were little glowing stars strategically placed along the ceiling and walls. A little planetarium. A little universe inside a larger one.

And as he was sure she would be, there she was in the doorway.

"Here, Scott," he said to the boy at his side. See how many constellations you can pick out." He then paced to the door to see Abigail.

"Hi," he said.

"Hi," she peeped.

"Can I see her now?"

"Not now, Abigail. You see, the sky is turning. At least it seems so because we are turning on earth. You would not be able to see her until about one in the morning."

"But I'll be in bed!"

"I'm sorry. I do not control the universe, Abigail. If you could come, we could see her."

"I'll sneak out!" she shrieked. "I only live a block from here!"

"Now Abigail, you know that would not be wise."

Abigail ran down the stairs. The telescope man followed her through the great eye of the scope as she drove home and went inside her house. Later, that evening, at 12:45, he was peering toward her bedroom window. He was sure she would not come, but was in the store to be on the safe side. He saw the sash go up in Abigail's cottage and Abigail climbed out.

"God all mighty," he sighed as he followed her to the store through the watchful eye of the telescope to be sure she was safe.

There was a small meteor shower in the west. More falling stars and wishes then most men could have in a lifetime. The telescope man wished the same wish on them all as Abigail was padding up the steps. He heard the footsteps as she neared his door.

"Come in," he said pleasantly.

Abigail sat obediently on the windowsill.

"Now," began the telescope man, "before we look for your sister we must be sure what we are looking for. I need you to tell me all about her so we know when you see her."

"She is seven years old. About this high." Abigail stretched her finger up to her sister's height. "She has blue eyes, kind of brown and blond hair and a little nose. She isn't fat or skinny. Just regular size. She smiles a lot."

"And her voice? If you were downstairs, and she wanted you right away, how would she call you?"

Abigail's face then brightened. "She'd say, 'Hey Abbie!' and then I would run up the steps."

"Okay. Remember those words and how she said them. Remember her face carefully. Where did she like to go more than anywhere else?"

"The beach."

"Doing what?"

"Looking shells."

The telescope man then began to peer through the scope. He slowly handed it to Abigail.

"The scope is pointed to heaven now. It's just beyond the stars over there. It will take your eyes a while to see it. But your eyesight will race through those stars and you will see it there. But you will only be able to see it for an instant. Heaven travels fast through the universe. When

I boost the scope to high power, it can only sustain the strain for but a moment."

Abigail peered out the scope and slid out of the store and into the universe. Past the moon. Past Saturn, Venus, and Mars. Past thousands of suns flew Abigail at lightning speed as she grabbed the scope hard so she would not fall down.

The words of the telescope man hovered like flying saucers over her head.

"Look hard for her Abigail, look very hard. And remember her. More than you ever have."

Abigail pictured Stephanie on the beach looking for shells. She was on her hands and knees sifting through the sand wearing her favorite blue bathing suit. Flecks of blue sparkled out from her squinting eyes, squinting out to Abigail about to call her over to show her a shell she just found. Like in slow motion Abigail saw her fill her lungs to call her over . . ."

"Now!" shouted the telescope man. And instantaneously the scope gave a low whine as it focused further into the universe and a bright strobe light went off in the store.

"Stephanie!" Abigail wailed. "It's me! Abigail! Stephanie!"

And it was over. Just the stars again as the scope whined back to earth. She turned and hugged the telescope man. She was sobbing.

"She's on the beach. She waved at me!"

"And she's okay?" he asked.

"Oh yes, she's fine," sobbed Abigail cheerfully, "but I think she misses me."

"I am sure she does," said the telescope man. "That is one of the mysteries of the universe. You see, we are all headed in different directions while going to the same place."

"What?"

"I just mean you will see her again."

"Tomorrow.?"

"No, I'm sorry. Heaven will not be in view for another hundred years. You are a very lucky girl to get a chance to see it."

Abigail was overcome with emotion. "Thank you sir. This is the nicest present I could ever have. I won't worry about her anymore."

"Now, this is our secret?"

"Oh, yes sir."

The telescope man followed Abigail home through his scope. He watched her cut over a dune and slide back in her window. She was safe now for sure. And happy. But the telescope man was troubled. Because there are a few things little girls are pretty good at: They can see what adults cannot, and they can let out a secret.

The telescope man looked glumly at his scope. "Is that where you are hiding?" he asked. He drove home in thought under the stars, went out to his porch, and stared at the sky for a long time.

At 8:30 the following evening Abigail's mother marched up the stairs to The Telescope Store. She was angry. No responsible adult tells a girl to sneak out of the house and then fills her head with nonsense!

She made a beeline for the store where the telescope man, as usual, was showing a boy a constellation.

"You sir!" she retorted sharply. "I would like to have a word with you!"

But when the telescope man turned around, he was not there. He was someone else. This was not the broad-shouldered man with the smoldering volcanic eyes. This was a kindly blue eyed man with glasses.

"Ma'am?" he replied.

"Where is the owner?"

"You mean professor Gallo."

"Professor?"

"Yes, he teaches at a university in the fall. Fascinating man. Studies astronomy, philosophy, psychology. Bright guy."

"Well, where is he? I would like a word with him," said Abigail's mother trying to maintain her anger.

"You know, it's a funny thing. He left this morning. Said he would send some students for the stuff. Went back to the university. Said something about crossing a line between imagination and reality. Said he hardly knew the difference anymore. Kind of talked like he was out of sorts. God knows he understood the imagination. He had this God given uncanny talent to capture a person's imagination. You could look through that scope of his at a planet and he would start telling you all about it and it was as if you could see every mountain range and valley he described. Was hard to tell the difference between what you saw through the scope and what you saw in your head. But it was always a beautiful thing, to look through the scope and listen to him. A very gentle nice guy. But looked shaken up. When I asked if something was wrong, he just said something about how people should be careful about gambling. But, ya know, I never saw him gamble."

Abigail's mother calmed down as she walked down the stairs along the waterfall. She remembered Abigail this morning. Happy. Confident about life. Going on about how Stephanie was okay just as her mother had said she was. What was the difference between what she told Abigail and what the telescope man did? She peered at the rainbow the waterfall was throwing out toward her. She bit her hand a little as she remembered Stephanie. God only knew where Stephanie was. And wherever she was, God was not returning her any time soon. But Abigail, in a manner of speaking, was gone too. Gone was the happy little child who would giggle herself to sleep. Who would wake up every morning with a smile on her face. She was gone; replaced with a despondent little girl who cried herself to sleep at night. Who sat forlornly with counselors while they tried to make her happy again. But she found no reason for happiness. Her sister was gone. The sister she played with every day and made her world sing. Stephanie was gone, and Abigail left with her.

But no longer. She was back. She laughed and smiled as she told of how she saw Stephanie on the beach. She was happy again. She was back, her little girl. It was the telescope man who gave her back. She knew she should be furious. But how could she be?

The man from the store was coming down the steps. He paused before her, but she said nothing. So he walked on. After a few steps he heard her call to him.

"Sir?"

He stopped and she walked over to him with emotion hitting her every which way.

"Tell him." She paused.

"Ma'am?"

"Tell him his gambling paid off. And, tell him Abigail's mother said thank you."

"Ma'am?"

"He'll understand."

Abigail's mother then let go of how it happened, this wonderful gift, or if the telescope man was responsible or irresponsible. She thought long and hard about the telescope man. She then looked at the heavens and said, at least tried to say, but she had a hard time voicing the words because of the tears that raced down her face purging her soul of sadness, "Was it you? Somehow?" she said in a small voice. "That had a hand in all this?" As she was trying to figure it out, before she could even think, the words "Thank you" came from her lips ever so slightly, barely audible, but some of the most important words she ever spoke. She floated them up to the sky, and like Abigail, she too, was changed and happy.

The story was over. But Sue was still in the story. There by the fountain catching the faint rainbows created by the mists of the waterfall. There gazing up to the window of The Telescope Store. Confused. Lost. Found.

Tom put the story down.

"Well?"

Sue was startled. This was not the voice of the story where she now belonged. This was Tom. She slowly came back from the fountain. To another story taking place in the back of a small retail store in North Carolina. She looked at him in a peculiar way.

"It's beautiful," she said. She took the story in her hands and ran her fingers through it as if to be sure it was real. She put it on a little stand by the bed. His hand brushed hers as he pulled the covers under his chin. It seemed this movement brushed away any awkwardness there could be to having her there in his bed. It was as natural as the breeze in the evening that his other hand swept her hair a little out of her face and he kissed her. She kissed him back and cradled back into his arm and neither remembered falling asleep.

Chapter 5

He woke up with her curled up in his arms like a kitten. He gave her a little shake as the dawn touched her cheek. He kissed her forehead lightly and she slowly, partially, opened her eyes.

"I'm awake. I'm going to the bakery for something to eat. I'll be back in a while."

He left. She caught his scent on the pillow and pulled it close. She blinked at the dawn, pulled the covers around her, and here, where she had never been before, felt like home.

That day he ran the store and she sat on the beach. The sun was warm as was the water. She went for a swim and took a nap. She thought of her marriage for a moment, but the thought could not stick. It was as if bad things did not happen here. She bought them tuna fish sandwiches for lunch and they ate them in the store as she helped some teenage girls put together some ear rings on a table Tom designed for people who wanted to create their own jewelry. There, there were beads of semi precious stones and all the parts to put together necklaces, ear rings, and ankle bracelets. Tom smiled secretly as Sue was having a big time with the girls.

Chapter 6

Later that evening they went out for dinner. Sue insisted she buy since, after all, she was getting a free place to stay at the beach. Tom knew better than to argue, so he went along for the ride. One thing he loved about Sue was her family was loaded and she was doing pretty well on her own, but she never asked for anything. Not even a hint of a dinner out. She was always happy just going to the beach or sitting around the apartment having a little meal as Tom would pick on the guitar.

When they returned about eleven o'clock, it was still balmy outside. The heat intrigued her. They decided to put on their bathing suits and go for a dip. Tom put a fine point on the word "dip." He was a surfer and was wary of sharks. He knew night time was not the best choice for swimming. She dove right in the water and laughed at Tom being hesitant. He soon dove in and quickly went for the beach and she followed. When he turned to look at her, he thought if the moonlight were personified, she would be the moonlight.

"Made it!" she said.

"That may be the last time for that nonsense. Gives me the willies."

Sue laughed. "You're probably right."

They walked back to their towels to pat off. The waves lapped gently onto the beach and the moon was cooperative. It provided just enough gravity to pull the tide slightly back and with it lift their hearts.

They both got ready for bed quickly and slipped into the covers.

Sue waited a minute and then said, "Hey, I'm getting gypped!"

"What are you talking about?"

"I want my bedtime story."

"What makes you think there are any more?"

"C'mon," she said as she pointed her thumb over to the folders on the shelf.

He frowned. "You may not like the next one."

"Let's find out."

He was a little apprehensive.

Sue slapped his arm. "C'mon. I came all the way from New Jersey to see you, and then buy you dinner, DINNER, Now you read me my story!"

Tom groaned as he went to the shelves and pulled out another folder.

"You're worse than a four-year-old."

It was true in a way, she thought. She had to play the businesswoman up north selling office furniture. She was good at it, but it was full of facades. Here she could be pampered and just be herself. She missed being treated like a little girl. She supposed all women did.

He got into bed, turned on the little pool of light on the page of the story, turned on his back and began to read.

"This one is called "The Immortal Dog.'"

"By Tom Johnson," she added in.

Tom laughed. "Yes, by Tom Johnson."

"Years ago there was a wizard in Canterbury," he began . . .

"Wait!" cried Sue.

Tom jumped a little. "What?"

Sue then took his right arm and pulled it beneath her and leaned comfortably into his shoulder. She scrunched around a little to get settled in. She then looked up at Tom.

"Okay. Now go."

Tom smiled gently toward her with all his defenses down. This unspoken gesture for Sue was a huge compliment to her. She smiled back. She kissed his arm and looked up at him.

"Ready?" said Tom.

"Ready," said Sue.

Chapter 7

THE IMMORTAL DOG

Years ago there was a wizard in Canterbury. It seems every trade has one individual who stands along at the top of his profession. The best chef, carpenter, physician, or whatever it may be. As for first class wizardry, no one could touch Latrom. If any other evil wizard turned a princess into a frog, or put a drought on the kingdom, it was always Latrom who could remove the spell in a jiff.

He had apprentices a plenty, as anyone who wanted to enter the wizard trade was sure to seek out Latrom. Not only was he the greatest wizard, but the wisest man in all the country. Even the king, though not publicly, but among trusted friends under the influence of mead, would speak how he would council with Latrom about problems in the kingdom.

Latrom never took credit for advice he gave the king. He had no political aspirations. He was too busy with his studies. Because Latrom believed to be a truly fine wizard, and a responsible one, Latrom thought he should learn all he could about the different sciences and philosophies of life.

But, though a wizard, Latrom was still just man, a very loved one by all who knew him, which Latrom cherished most of all in his life, but there was always something missing from his life. The age-old question of what was to face him after mortality plagued him to the point where he could not even enjoy his life any longer. He was one hundred and twenty years old now, but had the looks and good health of a man of sixty. But even all his clean honest wizard living and incantations of youth could not keep him going forever

A very special pleasure he did have in his life, however, was his faithful dog Wonrof. Day in, and day out, Wonrof would stretch in the morning after waking, immediately wag his tail, enjoy breakfast, and rest his big head, full of love and life, on Latrom's lap. Toward the afternoon, Latrom would throw a stick for Wonrof until he would tire, never of the game, but of physical fatigue. This Latrom would always know because Wonrof would return the stick and serenely place it at Latrom's feet and cover it with his paw as if to say, "Enough is enough, now let's enjoy the sun and the sky." Latrom would then lay on the grass with Wonrof's head resting on his lap. Latrom would sometimes ponder at this time, other times he would just enjoy the view, and sometimes fell into a little nap.

The wizard learned much from Wonrof. Wonrof seemed to always be happy. He ate when he was hungry and played when he was frisky, and slept when he was tired. He seemed to be in touch with how his body functioned, and never fought off its wishes. It seemed a good way to be to Latrom, as Wonrof's spirit was always fed well by his content constitution.

As for love, Wonrof was full. Full of love for Latrom, the flowers and the birds. As for the ladies, when they came along, he would pursue his carnal pleasures; it was his nature. He accepted base pleasures for what they were. He was never fooled, however, into believing that the pretty tail of a Setter or the long lashes of a Cocker were any more than they were. He certainly admired the ladies; but he knew this emotion was not to last: it was not love. Love was his head on Latrom's knee by the fireside while he was sighing his doggie sighs or dreaming his doggie dreams.

Tom could not help it right now. He looked down at Sue who was resting comfortably on his shoulder. Sue looked up and smiled.

'I'm not a dog, you know.' She then nestled even more comfortably toward Tom.

'Go on,' she said.

Tom took a breath and returned to the story.

As Latrom and Wonrof grew older, Wonrof never seemed to grow unhappy. He began to have some of life's little health problems, but as soon as he recovered from a strain of the hip or a tad of indigestion, he was perfectly happy once again. He did not run after the ladies the way he used to. He would laugh and shake his head when he saw the younger dogs chasing tail all over the kingdom. But if amour passed his way, he certainly would enjoy it. He was never sad, except when his great friend Latrom was in a particularly pensive mood, absorbed with life's perplexities.

One winter night when the fire was cozy and Latrom was particularly pensive, Wonrof gave a soft sigh and licked the hand of his dear friend. The wizard looked down and love filled his heart for his old companion, and he said, "Faithful Wonrof, why is it you are always so happy. What is your secret?"

It was then that a dark mood came over Latrom as he peered into Wonrof's brown trusting eyes. It was all night long that Latrom poured over his magical books in his far reaching catacombs. He finally found what he was looking for and sighed in relief and desperation.

That morning, when Wonrof was stretching, the wide, wide book lay there on the table. Wonrof noticed his food was a bit on the unpalatable side, but he did not complain, as was his way. As he finished, Latrom looked longingly at his old friend. He stroked his broad forehead and recited some bazaar lyrical words Wonrof had never heard before. On the table were two sticks: the one Wonrof recognized as his favorite stick and another one. The other was strange and mystical and Wonrof did not recognize it.

Everything was done, thought Latrom. The strange ingredients he rarely touched from the long, dark depths of caverns, from high on mountain tops, and from deep in the sea, ingredients most men had never laid their eyes on, were put in just the right proportion for Wonrof. The lyrical spell was said. Now all that was left was to break the magical stick. At that point, if he did not know already, Wonrof would know for sure, that there was death. He would know that as each day melted into the other, there would be a day when there would be no more days. There would be some type of end. And as how the end would be: there could be doubt.

Out they went and Latrom threw Wonrof's favorite stick as far as he could down a ravine. As Wonrof happily chased it, Latrom took out the mysterious stick, pointed it at Wonrof, said some strange words, and then broke it over his knee.

At that Wonrof stood dead in his tracks. A new emotion poured over him. He looked up at the sky in wonder, all of the sudden realizing it could pass. The butterflies and the hop toads, too. And what of his friend Latrom? He gazed over his shoulder and his deep brown eyes filled with tears. He then lay down and moaned a long howl into the soft wind. He began to think of all the ladies in his life and how much all their acquaintances meant to him, and how that too would at one time be no more. He then jumped up in a panic and ran out of the ravine and over a hill. Latrom called and called, but Wonrof was not to return.

Now that life was short, Wonrof was ready to live it all as quickly as possible. He saw a pretty Cocker Spaniel. Hours before, he would have cast her a nonchalant gaze and been on his way, caring not for her opinions. But could this be his last chance for love? The word crossed Wonrof's mind in a queer way. Love, he thought, since when was this love? But he could not help it. The desperation of his short life swept over him like a storm surge. Finally, through subtle passes and brave tricks he had not performed in years, he was accepted as a lover of the Cocker.

But upon a short rest after their affair, the Cocker got up and went on her merry way. At this Wonrof sighed a cry because he knew his time was limited and he may never enjoy such pleasures again. He walked away burdened as if under a great weight. What should one do, when it could be one's last chance to do it? Before, Wonrof was patient. There would always be another day to complete any doggie dream he dreamed. But now, what if he died before all his dreams could be completed? His eyes filled with tears again, and his heart with loneliness as his thoughts turned to his old friend Latrom.

What of Latrom? he thought. Would, there, could there, be an end to their long beautiful nights by the fire? The warmth of Latrom's hand on his brow? The comfort of using Latrom's foot for a pillow? The lazy way he would softly fall asleep at Latrom's feet knowing he would wake again to see his dear friend? Could it be that that too would be gone? He stood up and let out a long brokenhearted howl as he gazed back over the hill where he had left Latrom.

And there he saw him. Latrom was running hard after Wonrof calling his name. At the sight of him, whimpering and crying, Wonrof ran desperately to Latrom. At least with him there would be love. This he did know. And Latrom could be gone one day. This he also knew.

When he finally reached Latrom, Wonrof fell to his feet and sobbed uncontrollably. Full of guilt, Latrom petted his great friend's head and moaned. "Oh what have I done? It was a cruel thing to do if only for a short time." The spell was only to last till the sun reached high noon. Latrom then stood taller than he ever stood, and called a spell louder than he ever did, that made the sun move ever so much faster until it reached its peak at noon, and then slowed back to its snail's pace.

"There, there, there you are, old friend," said Latrom. Wonrof was still sobbing, but more controllably now. Slowly, and then quickly, the pain left Wonrof's face and a faint smile curled over his lips as he gazed up at his old friend Latrom that was surely his friend forever.

"There you go," whispered Latrom as he kissed Wonrof's head. And all was forgiven, all was forgotten, and all was forever.

And Latrom too, for the first time in years, smiled a big smile as he hugged his lovely friend. "For all the doubt and uncertainty, we do have this great love of ours, don't we?"

And just at that moment Latrom forgot about his own mortality and watched the butterflies and the bees blissfully as he petted his good and faithful friend. Through his great love for Wonrof, Latrom too, had achieved immortality: if only for a moment.

Tom finished the story and waited as he did before. And as the night before, nothing. Sue was enamored by the story. Lost in its confusion but somehow saved by it.

"Well," he said.

She shook her head. "It's beautiful. Like last nights. A little scary, but wonderful too."

She looked up at Tom. "Another keeper," she said with a smile.

This little praise from Sue was similar to the smile he had given her earlier. She nestled into Tom's arm and they fell asleep. About one in the morning, they for some reason both awoke. They said nothing as they began to kiss. They had done this before when they used to spend the night together years ago. It was wonderful then; it was wonderful now, as the moon lulled near the horizon, and the world as Tom and Sue knew it for the moment was full of a kind rhythm that created a song they thought they would never hear again, and then they softly fell back to sleep.

The next day, Sue woke before Tom. She looked over at his face and kissed it. She began to cry a little. She did not want to be alone and shook him awake.

When Tom woke up, he saw Sue was crying. "I don't want to go," she whimpered. Tom had never seen Sue like this before. He reached out for her and drew her toward him and kissed her forehead. "You don't have to until tomorrow," he said, trying to comfort her, but he knew what she meant.

They showered and dressed and tried to put leaving out of their minds. Mary Ann would be watching the store that day so they had time to play. They went to the beach. Tom let Sue ride a few waves in on his raft and later paddled out further to catch the bigger surf on his surfboard. They sat lazily under a beach umbrella and let the breeze keep them cool and slow their hearts. For lunch they had some veggie sandwiches on a bench outside his store. For fun, Sue went in and talked to Mary Ann as she helped some women decide on some jewelry and put together a nice pair of earrings for the daughter of one of the women at the jewelry table. Sue had impeccable taste, and somehow the people in the store quickly picked up on that and trusted her judgment. Again, Tom smiled inwardly as he watched Sue enjoying herself.

It was his turn to treat for dinner. He took her to a restaurant called Penguin Isle which was run by a friend of his, Tom Sloate. It overlooked the bay and at night wild foxes would run through its yard. It was their last night and neither mentioned it when they climbed into bed.

"Okay," said Sue brightly, trying to not worry about tomorrow, "fire it up."

"I won twice. Maybe I should quit while I am ahead."

Sue just sneered at him.

"All right, All right," said Tom as he took another story off the shelf.

Sue immediately pulled his arm around him and nestled into his shoulder.

"This one is called "Honk."

"Honk?"

"Honk."

"By Tom Johnson?"

"Yes," he laughed lightly, "by Tom Johnson."

"Okay." Sue then kissed his shoulder. "Go Ahead."

Chapter 8

Honk

It was the fall, and he was not used to the town. It was far inland where the trees lost their leaves, falling like small memories of summer. He marveled at them in a curiously sad way as they lay on the ground. Such passages of the seasons were different in his town, Nags Head, off the coast of North Carolina. There, the Atlantic dropped slowly in temperature in the fall, one degree at a time, as the sun disappeared sooner every day signaling the cool northwest winds to blow along the sand accompanied by the monarch butterflies that appeared in the fall as if for no reason. He supposed it was nature's way of giving the beach falling leaves. And fall had arrived. Most of the tourists had migrated away beneath the long delta wings of the geese.

It was there they met. She had just graduated from college and was working as a cocktail waitress at Kelly's restaurant. He was in the same restaurant working as a waiter. It was fun for him at first, to live on an island and wait tables. It was his way of being a kind of expatriate, but it was getting old. He began to miss teaching school and the culture the inland offered. But he loved the beach: he always did, but life was beginning to get complicated. How long should he remain?

She, on the other hand, was peeking out at the world as a fawn peers out at the lights on a highway. There were no grade point averages out here. No one cared about any of that. It was all profits and losses, and how much money you could hustle from your last table where you served drinks. It was unnerving to her, but she was pleasant enough about it. She never raised her voice and was a bit too slow for most of the waiters. But he took a fancy to her demeanor. He enjoyed watching her pad along with a look of determination on her face as she struggled to remember who got which martini.

One evening he asked her if she wanted to take a small tour of the island. She said she would, and they met after work for her tour. He liked the slow way she turned her head to look at the sights and the sky. And he liked her impish smile as she gave a small gasp when she saw a raccoon or some such nocturnal creature in the night.

And he liked the way she would tilt her head to look up at the stars as if she was putting along in the middle of the universe in his little Karmann Ghia. And actually, when he thought about it, they were. Since if the universe was forever, everyone, everywhere was at the center of it, if they chose to think of it that way.

He drove through the night toward a national park. There were no streetlights here, and the stars came out to show what the sky was like back in prehistoric times. He drove down a long road to Bodie Island lighthouse that blinked on and off. There was one house there, where the caretaker of the lighthouse lived, and that was all. The moon was pinned up low over the trees. The constellations, faceless, but not without souls, called to him to show them off to Emily. He pointed out Orion, the Dippers, Cassiopeia, and the Seven Sisters.

They stood silently enjoying the view and then turned toward one another. He didn't kiss her there. He thought it would be unfair to her if his intentions were not reciprocated; here, in the middle of nowhere, where it seemed only somewhere existed. But when he dropped her off at her house where she had a graceful exit, he kissed her. He kissed her for a long while as she reached up toward his shoulders to draw him in.

As their rides grew longer, their acquaintance grew stronger, and they became very fond of one another. They offered no form of commitment; they stayed together for one simple reason: they enjoyed one another's company.

As the summer rolled along, they became more and more comfortable with each other. She loved to hear him play his guitar and sing softly in the moonlight. She remembered the first time she asked him to play and was a little skittish. What if he were terrible? But he wasn't. He played beautifully and purposefully along with a nice gentle voice. She had fallen asleep many evenings while listening to him play. When she apologized for being rude, he said "I'm happy my music relaxes you." She smiled then and kissed his cheek.

They would love to blow up their rafts and ride the waves together. She would smile her funny smile when she thought she caught a big wave; and he would laugh beyond the breakers because to him the waves were very small. When they got bigger, he would take his board and go surfing as she would lie on the beach and watch, nap, and snack on something they would throw together from Billy's Seafood grocery store.

They would request the same section in the back of the restaurant and work it together. The section was small, which was why they liked it. They would joke around until the customers came in. Then they would do their best bringing the salads, entrees, drinks, deserts, and finally coffees to the tables. The customers always enjoyed them even if she made a mistake here and there.

At the end of the night they would go to his house, take showers, and go outside with a gin and tonic and watch the moon stroll about the sky until they tired. They would then go inside and curl up under the covers as the air conditioner kept the humidity and warm air out of his apartment. They would not think of the restaurant under the quilt. They would not really think of anything in particular. They would just nestle up to one another and enjoy falling asleep.

During the day he used to love to watch her eyes grow wide, like a pretty Disney character when she would forget something on their camping trip. He always forgave her, but poked a little fun at her because he enjoyed the expression on her face when she was a bit upset with herself. She would finally laugh and say, "Oh Honk, we didn't need that old pan anyway." She would then give him a funny look and take his arm. "No, Donk, we like cold canned things," he would say and they would laugh together. Honk and Donk. Their ridiculous pet names. A silly game they played. Neither could remember where the names came from or even who was supposed to be Honk or Donk.

But that summer was over now. The oceans and continents had all circled the sun quite a few times since then. They kept up. Dated other people. Hurt one another with life's hurts. And out of nowhere, grew distant.

He was not expected. His feet rustled through the leaves toward her door. She was doing fine, she thought. She was making a nice living in a comfortable town. He tapped on the door. She opened it, and her face fell back to the sea, the rafts, the balmy nights on the coast. His hair had turned a bit grey along the temple, she noticed, but his face was kind and gentle as she had remembered it.

She reached out and hugged him, and he ran his fingers down her silky hair and his thumb stroked her smooth cheek. She moved slowly and deliberately with a touch of caution as she always had. They never really ever broke up, they just moved further away through time and space. So they talked little nonsense talk. She invited him in, but he said he had to go. He lied and she knew it. He was a terrible liar. But the truth was that it hurt him to stay. How could they continue this charade that they may be together once more? They walked to his car, and as he was about to get in he said, "Well, Honk, I guess this is kind of final. Guess we knew one day it would be."

His face grew sad and his heart ached at the words she only half believed. He always wondered what the words would sound like. They sounded terrible. He only saw her cry one time before. This was the second time. He was in the car, but the window was rolled down. She held onto his arm as if it were a lever to switch the universe off so she could keep him there forever. She sobbed a little sob and lightly kissed his ear and rubbed her cheek on his hand to brush a tear away.

"I can't say that," she whimpered. "It's all too sweet." But it was all too absurd. She was seeing someone else right now, and he felt he had no right to interrupt. He pulled his arm in the window. "Well, I best go, Donk."

She didn't utter a word. He methodically put the car in drive and rolled over the fallen leaves under the long tree branches that were so unfamiliar to him. The leaves crackled a soft song under his tires to try to soothe his now aching heart, but though they tried to help him, they could not help much. He did not look back; she did not take her eyes off the car until it rounded the curve and disappeared from sight.

"Bye Donk," she whispered thinly through her lips as she sat down on the curb and reached down to crackle some leaves in her hands that sang the same soft song they sang to him as he drove away. But the song did not help her either; it only made her more sad.

Because the song was pretty, and she liked it; and she knew now that it would always remind her of what was now leaving her life. And not even the October moon that loomed over the trees, could fill her now lonely heart. And big and lonely as the moon, came some tears that fell and patted down on the fallen leaves.

One, for the comfort they both had; one for the love they either never had, or never knew they had; one for the love they never admitted to having; and the last one, the one that would return late at night on odd occasions, was for the love they had for one another that was lost in their heart, and that they were afraid of.

Tom finished the story. Sue was lightly silent by his side.

"I hated that one," she said.

She then talked into his arm. "And who is this stupid Donk anyway?"

"It's just a story."

"I don't believe you."

Time passed.

"Don't you ever do that to me."

"What?"

"Say it's over, even if you think it is, don't you dare say it."

"I would never say that to you, Sue."

"Just be sure you don't," she said.

She then went into the bathroom and washed her face so Tom would never be able to tell she cried at the ending. Upon coming out she said, "Is this all there is, this long weekend?"

"I don't want it to be."

"Good!" she said and jumped on the bed and straddled him. "That's better! Now you get that damn Honk or Donk out you your head, you understand? And get me in there." She grabbed his head and shook it. "I am claiming this stupid head!"

Tom laughed as she shook his head. She then leaned down and kissed him.

Chapter 9

He was all the way to the gate where he could go no further. They had only discussed her leaving once before and never mentioned it again.

"I still don't want to go," she said.

Tom drew her near and held her; she held him tightly and breathed a breath to keep her composed. This was not like her and she fought it, but not very well. "What the hell is going on here?" she mumbled.

"I'm not sure, but I wonder, if we weren't such asses, if we could have fallen in love this weekend."

"I'm really not an ass, you know," she said into his shoulder. "I mean I know YOU are."

"Well, I'm not if you're not," he said evenly. He then did a terrible thing. He pushed her away. Why was he pushing her away?

"You'll miss your flight," he said evenly. She looked at the clock and wanted to spit on it. How did it dare take her away?

"Say it first," she demanded.

"I'll say it. I'll say it first just to prove once and for all I am braver than your little chicken ass. I love you Sue. I always have."

He then reached out and touched her nose.

"So there," he said.

"Me too. But just like that story . . . Let's not be that awful story!"

"We can write our own from here."

She tore herself away and walked halfway down to the plane. She turned.

Tom was still watching her. "I'll MISS you," she said, and ran to the plane trying not to look like a fool.

Sue walked onto the plane and didn't look back. Tom turned to leave.

"Keep it quick and uncomplicated," they both said inside their heads.

Sue found a spot for her bag and pushed it into the compartment and sat down. She then looked out over the airport in Virginia, thinking back to the ocean breezes of North Carolina a hundred or so miles away, and Tom walking to his car. The stories, the swim, his smile, and most of all lying there being read to with his arm around her floating in the pool of light visiting a lovely dog, a wizard, and a child. Waking up before him watching him sleep. All this as the door to the plane was secured, and the plane rolled a few feet toward the runway.

Sue got up quickly and ran to the door.

"I have to get off," she said curtly in her business façade.

"Maam, the door has been secured. We can't let you off now."

"The DOOR is right there."

"It's secured."

"You better let me off this damn plane."

"We can't let you do that now, it's against regulations. We've left the airport."

"IT'S right there, just back up!"

"Back up?" The stewardess looked at her with a, *Did she just say back up?* expression on her face.

"I bet you would let a terrorist off this plane!"

"Well of course."

"Then I am a terrorist. I am going to do something really mean in here!"

The other stewardess quickly went to cabin.

"Now maam, calm down."

"I mean it. I'll, I'll, go into the bathroom and light up and smoke, I will!" Sue fumbled inside her pocketbook for some cigarettes she hid in her tampon container.

"See there," she waved two Marlboros under the stewardess's nose. "Evidence," she proclaimed proudly. The door then opened and two security guards were there standing on portable stairs that were rolled to the plane.

"Uh oh," said Sue.

"Come with us please," said two uniformed officers.

Tom was just getting back to the highway when his cell phone rang.

"Hello, Tom Johnson?"

"Yes, and who would this be please?"

"Airport security. Would you know a Sue Coburn?"

"Yes," Tom began a small panic. "Is she alright?"

"Yes sir, she is, she is right here."

"What happened to the plane?"

"It departed."

"But I put her on the plane. She was walking to the gate when I left. She did get on it didn't she?"

"Yes sir, but she refused to stay on it."

Tom could hear Sue in the back round whining, "Let me talk to him. This is my phone call right? You should give me *that* phone!" The security guard then gave her a look that shut her yap quick.

"Please, please give me the phone."

He handed her the phone, and she bent down and cupped her hand and whispered to Tom.

"I'm in a hell of a lot of trouble. And it's all YOUR fault!"

"My fault?! What did I do?"

"*What did I do?*" she mocked. "Look, apparently I broke a couple of laws."

"What the? What have you done?!"

"Um, threatened I was going to smoke on the plane?"

"You don't smoke."

"Well, about that, we'll get to that later."

"You smoke?"

"Later I *SAID* and a couple of other things, too."

"What? Like what?"

"Um, she whispered in the phone, "like I told them I was a terrorist?"

"A WHAT!? Have you lost your mind?!"

"Well I had to do SOMETHING. It's the only way I could get off the plane. I know it was stupid. I'll never do it again. I panicked. I just didn't want to go," she said and her eyes began to well up with some tears. "Look, you gotta substantiate my story and bust me *outta* here."

"Bust you outta there?"

"Yea, bust me OUTTA here. I mean the coppers have me and everything!"

"The coppers?" Tom began to laugh a little. "You are a lotta trouble, you know that?"

"I don't MEAN to be," she said in a small childish way.

"You are unbelievable," said Tom with a smile on his face. "Don't worry, I'll come and get you."

"Yes," she said, and she rubbed her finger up and down the phone like it was the dearest thing in her whole life. "You do that," she said. "You come and get me."

Chapter 10

Tom explained the best he could what was going on to the officers, and with the help of some female officers who were present, who were there to try to explain how women think, they bought the story and let Sue go after taking all of her personal information. They walked out of the airport, with Sue not knowing what to say. When they finally got in the car, Tom leaned over and kissed her. It was the nicest of kisses, but Sue was ashamed of herself.

"Don't think I stayed for you is all. I just wanted to have some more time off is all," she lied.

"Okay," smiled Tom.

"I can get a hotel you know."

"I know."

Silence for a moment.

"Are you going to sit there and let me get a hotel?!" she demanded.

"I don't want you too, but if you . . ."

"*I don't want you too,*" she mocked. "Look dufus, this is what you say, you moron, you say, 'Sue, please stay with me. Don't go to a hotel.'"

"Please stay with me, Sue, Don't go to a hotel, how's that?"

"Not very good," pouted Sue.

"Of course you will stay with me, Sue. And that phone call, although bazaar, was fine with me. I am delighted to have you back."

"And you want me to stay because . . . ."

"Because . . . ?" inquired Tom

"Because you love me. Did you not say that at the airport?"

"I said that."

"But did you mean that?"

"I said it didn't I?"

Sue grabbed Tom's arm and began to pinch it harder and harder.

"Say what I want to hear!"

"I meant it! I meant it! Criminey you have nails you know."

"That's right, and I know how to use them," warned Sue as she gave him a funny stern look and waved her nails in front of his face. "So you just better watch out!"

Tom then drew her over toward him and she put her head on his shoulder and fell asleep on the way to what she felt was home. Home to where she felt loved and cared for. And she would care for him too, she thought, as she drifted to sleep.

There were no stories that night. Just the two of them tired and happy to be together as they fell asleep in one another's arms. There by the sea, under the stars, beneath the cool breeze of the air conditioner and lying under Tom's quilt, which would, for a time, keep the monsters of how complicated life can be away from them for now.

Chapter 11

They awoke happily, Tom had the morning off, and the waves were good: about three feet or so, and Tom blithely rode one after the other as Sue watched in fascination. From time to time she went for a dip and stretched and read a magazine on the beach and made a few calls to the office and then put it out of her mind. It was the laziest of days and Tom and Sue ran the shop that evening while Sue made some snacks in the back and offered them to Tom and the customers. She laughed with the women and teenage girls as she rang up the sales smirking at Tom as to what a good job she was doing. Tom smiled, and gave her a thumbs up.

At the end of the night, they locked the door and were ready to get a bite to eat. The warm air nestled around Sue. "Hey," she said, "we took in seven hundred bucks. I figure at a cost percentage of 33% over all and, oh, the cost of the rent, you raked in about three hundred clams."

She then held out her hand. "I want my one my buck fifty."

"You want. It's my store."

"You sat on your ass. I made all the sales."

"You were great. I admit it. I will compromise with you and buy you a nice dinner."

"And read me a story tonight?"

"Allright, allright. I have a few left. Will that settle it?"

"Maybe," she said.

Sue then looked around. The moon was a crescent, the stars winking, Tom smiling that, 'You are a pain in the ass smile.' She just got done work and loved it.

"I could get used to this," she said. She was testing the water.

"You just keep making me money, and I could get used to it too."

Sue stepped on Tom's foot. "That's not what I meant, and you know it!" She grabbed his ear and twisted it. "Say something nice, you jackass!"

"Hey, hey I need that frikkin ear!"

"Say it!"

"Let me go first."

She pulled her hand away as Tom rubbed his ear and Sue stood there tapping her foot.

"You are gorgeous," smiled Tom

"And."

"Intelligent and a great help here. And before you say "and" again. I could get used to it too. I already have. I still love you and even more so than yesterday."

Sue pulled him toward her and hugged him and whispered in his ear. "I love you too. Even more than this morning. And I am thinking how that scares me, and I am thinking I should not tell you that scares me. And just to really scare me I will tell you this too. I now know what love is. I never knew it until now. And I hate you. I hate you so much because you flew me through the milky way up to paradise and let me take a good look, and maybe one day I will have to leave. Maybe it won't last. And that is all *your* fault. So anyway, I take all this back, and I don't love you, but you have to still love me, you can't take it back. So there."

Tom laughed. "If that makes you happy, that's fine with me."

"It doesn't make me happy, but that is how it will be."

"You are a nut."

"Well, then that is your new problem. You are in love with a nut."

"And happy to be so."

Chapter 12

They had a nice dinner at Goombays celebrating a good take in the store. They laughed and talked business. What was selling, what wasn't, how they could merchandise things better. Sue came up with some great ideas, and Tom listened. Tom said he would appreciate it if she went through the catalogs looking for jewelry that she thought would sell.

"Sure," she said, "but it'll cost ya."

"Cost me what?"

"Let's see. A big shot like me doing consulting . . ."

"Oh, brother, we'll discuss it tomorrow."

"No, we'll discuss it now. You pay for this dinner. And tomorrow night, since I know you can afford it, we will go to that Penguin Isles again. On the store of course."

"On the store is on me."

"I know, dumbass, but since it is my pay you can write it off."

"I never thought of that."

"You just let me do the thinnin around here Baba Looey."

Tom laughed a good laugh and they headed back to the store to go to bed. Tom was in the covers and Sue slid in next to him. She snuggled under his arm and yawned.

"Get it," she said.

"It's right here princess. This one is a bit more lighthearted. It was actually written for kids around the sixth grade or junior high or something. But I think parents could enjoy it too, if that makes any sense at all."

"What if you're not a parent. Just like me?"

"I don't know. You tell me when it is over.

"Okay writer dude. Let her rip"

Chapter 13

SURFER GIRLS

For many people it is hard to believe that there is someone who has never seen the ocean. But Billy Barnard and Timmy Johnson were two who never have. They were both in the seventh grade and had been friends since the second grade. They lived around the corner form each other and were inseparable, or at least always knew where one another was. If you wanted to find Billy, just ask Timmy, and vice versa.

They both played soccer, Billy being the captain of the team and Timmy one of its lead scorers. They also were on the summer swim team there, where Timmy was the captain, and swam the lakes and rivers in Arkansas. They would love anything to do with the water: water skiing, kayaking, white water rafting, you name it. Their parents nicknamed them "the turtles," because they both seemed to need to be wet somewhere. But the one thing they had never done, was to swim in the ocean; but this was about to change.

It was a Monday night that Billy's dad took out a map of the United States and showed it to Billy and Timmy. He pointed to a strange little point of land one could barely see off of the coast of North Carolina.

"See it," he said. "A strange place. Not the usual beach town. Found it on the web. It's supposed to have the best surf on the East Coast."

At this Billy and Timmy's heart began to pound. *Surfing.* It was the one water sport they never had an opportunity to do. They loved it the first time they saw it in a movie they rented called *The Endless Summer.* They then rented every movie they could find about the subject: *Endless Summer 2, Point Break, Big Wednesday,* and on and on.

"Wanna go?" smiled Billy's dad. "Timmy can come. We cleared it with his parents."

Billy and Timmy could hardly speak. Their mouths just hung open and they just stood there.

"Well, do you want to go or not?" repeated Mr. Barnard.

"Yes!" they both chimed in as they looked at one another with smiles broad as the moon across their faces.

"We're gonna go surfin, SURFIN!!" Timmy said. Billy smiled broad as the equator and was so excited he could only go up to his dad and hug him. Mr. Barnard was happy he made this plan, figuring it would go well, but delighted it did. He loved these two kids. How couldn't he? Billy then hugged Mrs. Barnard, who hugged him back, realizing somehow, although it seemed impossible, there was actually a way to love this kid even more every day she knew him.

The trip was on. They flew into the airport in Norfolk, Virginia, which was about ninety miles from Nags Head, the town they would stay in on the Outer Banks of North Carolina. They arrived about 9:00 at night and rented a car to take to the beach. On the ride down they went through farmland covered by bright stars and a quarter moon. As they neared the bridge to go over the island, they sensed the salt air and both the boys stared in wonder at the size of the bay they were crossing. As they drove to find their cottage on the beach, Timmy jumped and punched Billy. There running sideways across the street was a little ghost crab. It was not the first one they were to see. They pulled up to the cottage which was right on the beach. It was tough for Billy's dad to afford the place, but he wanted the boys to be able to enjoy the ocean when they wanted. Plus, it would be a romantic spot for him and his wife Pat. That certainly helped in the decision. Not only that, Timmy's father insisted to offer to pay part of the rent and gave money for expenses for Timmy.

As soon as they got to the cottage, Timmy and Billy jumped out of the car and ran to the ocean. It was dark so they could not see it well, but its expanse was outlined by the stars that encompassed the sky and seemed to cradle the ocean in their hands. There was a low bass sound, the sound of the waves breaking off of the beach. Timmy and Billy stood silently at the edge of it and listened. They stood as if they were in the presence of royalty, and they were. This is where all water sought to be. The rain, the rivers, all of it came home here. It was the ocean that ruled the water. And water ruled the planet.

Neither said anything. Billy saw Timmy pulling off his shoes and did the same. Timmy looked over at Billy and counted.

"One, two, THREE!" and they both ran to the ocean and were knocked back on their butts by the shore break. They got up and dove over the first wave and came up wide eyed.

Timmy was licking at his lips. "You taste that?"

"Salt," Billy said, and they both smiled.

"Timmy! Billy! Get out of there! I didn't bring you both down there to get killed the first night we arrive!"

Billy and Timmy ran up to Mr. Barnard apologizing excitedly all the way. Mr. Barnard was not as mad as he was worried, but understood their excitement.

"Listen. This is new territory for you boys. You take it slow and use your heads. This is not a lake or a river you know. You need to learn its currents and ways just the way you learned the ways of the rivers you swim back home."

"Okay," they both said.

"I'm adamant about this. You be careful here. Now go put the bags in the house."

It was then that Pat walked up to Mr. Barnard and took his hand. They had been to the beach a few times before. Once was on their honeymoon. Mrs. Barnard put her hand around Mr. Barnard's waist and Mr. Barnard put his arm around his wife's shoulders.

"Damn fool kids," he muttered.

"Like their father," sighed Mrs. Barnard, "whom I love very much."

Mr. Barnard smiled and kissed his wife's forehead.

It was dawn when Timmy and Billy ran down to the beach. The sun rose above it like a great Greek medallion. Pelicans skimmed the water like prehistoric flying reptiles as the breeze lightly crossed their foreheads.

"Oh my God!" They both gasped as a porpoise jumped high into the air and then fell back to the sea where it swam along with its family gracefully arching above the water to gather its next breath.

"Oh my God!" they both said again. They looked at one another and were so happy they thought they would both burst. They had both seen porpoises in the movies but could never imagine how graceful they were in the water. It was as if they could both sense their intelligence.

Billy socked Timmy. "We're not in Kansas anymore, Toto," he said.

"Or Arkansas," replied Timmy.

As soon as they could figure out where the first surf shop was, they rented some boards. The boards stood in the shop as if they were the guardians of the ocean. There was the faint smell of fiberglass that filled their senses. They did not let on they were complete beginners to the owner, not wanting to seem like they were not cool. They said they had surfed "a couple of times." The owner rented them two boards about eight feet long. They were not fiberglass, they were made of a foam so if the board hit them, they would not get hurt. They both complained to Mr. Barnard they wanted real boards. Mr. Barnard said to first get the hang of it and he would see. They said okay. Well, they were boards nevertheless, they thought. They strapped the boards on the car with huge smiles. They felt like they had never seen anything as beautiful as the boards in that shop in their lives. At least not yet.

"You know," said Tom.

"What?" asked Sue, wondering why he interrupted the story.

"I should have had them sign up for surfing school here. It is the safe thing to do. But if I did, I couldn't get them to meet the surfer girls the way I wanted."

"So?"

"It just bothers me."

"Okay. Okay Mr. Safety. I get it. You got two excellent swimmers with a safety brochure on rented SOFT surfboards. Maybe you should have a disclaimer or something in the beginning of the book," she said jokingly.

"Maybe I just will."

"Alright, *whatever!*" said Sue with aggravation. "I am WAITING to hear the rest of the story if you don't mind. Now c'mon."

"Okay. Here we go."

Sue then smiled as she nestled into his chest to see what would happen next as Tom continued to read the story:

They were about to get into the ocean with their boards as they had seen in the movies when over the dune came two girls, Jackie and

Keaton. One was in the sixth grade, the other in the seventh. Both were athletes: swimmers, soccer players, and surfers. Neither had an ounce of fat on them and they both had long sun streaked hair. They looked like little mini supermodels as the walked down the beach. Keaton was a little taller than Jackie. Jackie had a rounder face than Keaton. They seemed to have an aura of pretty innocence that surrounded them. They laughed at one another as they walked to the water. They had a grace in their walk: They belonged to the sea. When they approached the waves, they nimbly jumped over the first wave of the shore break neatly landing on their boards and stroked to the surf. They were as fluid as the dolphins as they paddled out. Now this, this, was the most beautiful thing the boys had ever seen.

They stood there like fools with their mouths open. It was Billy who finally spoke.

"Surfer girls," was all he could say.

It wasn't that Billy and Timmy have not seen plenty of cute girls in their day. There were more than one sleep over when girls would swoon and talk about them both. The most popular girls in the school kept Billy and Timmy under their watchful eye along with all the other girls. And all the girls loved them. Not because they were good looking and athletic, although that helped, but because they were nice to everyone. Their parents raised them that way. It did not matter if you were the most popular girl in the school or a girl who liked to keep to herself, if a girl dropped her books, Timmy or Billy would help her pick them up.

One time Timmy caught John Holiday teasing Barbara Ward about being a little overweight, as some girls will get before they begin to grow. He saw her defend herself with dignity and then caught her crying around the corner. Timmy went up to John and shoved him hard.

"I oughta sock ya!" he said.

"What?" croaked John.

"You lay off Barbara."

"Okay, okay, don't get nuts about it. I was just having some fun."

"Well, find another way to have fun!" he said.

They finally made it out, a little further in than Keaton and Jackie, and they looked at them every time they could without being caught. It was Jackie that stroked into the first wave. She jumped up fearlessly, as she always did, and began to cut right toward Billy. Billy paddled hard for the wave, not knowing he was cutting Jackie off. He caught the wave, tried to stand up and fell off to the side. Jackie had to wipe out so she wouldn't hit him. She came up mad as fire as she stroked toward Keaton.

"Did you see what that jerk did?" she said.

"Yeah, said Keaton, what a touron."

Touron was what the locals called tourists who did stupid things. It was a combination of the word tourist and moron. When a surfer catches a wave, they will either go across the wave to the right or to the left. The surfer closest to the curl has the right of way and no one else should take the wave. The unwritten rules of surfing say you let the person in the best position in the wave, have it.

"The jerk dropped right in on me. I'll let that one go, but he'd better watch it!"

Keaton took the next wave. She stood up tall, straight, and graceful, as she always did, and rode the wave to the beach under the watchful eye of Billy and Timmy.

The next wave was perfect. A nice four footer coming right to Jackie. She was excited. The wave was a little bigger than most she was used to since there was a hurricane brewing far off the coast. She stood up quickly and hit her turn harder than Keaton. Jackie's style was compact and sharp. She just made her bottom turn, was about to crouch for the tube when: There he was again! Taking off on her! To avoid hitting him she had to straighten out and the wave pummeled her around and around. It was a tough wipe out and she was lit up. She came up and glared around for Billy. She saw him coming up since, as usual, he wiped out. She swam a bee line for him. He was just getting on his feet in waste deep water when he saw her swim up to him and get on her feet. But he wasn't on his feet for long. She shoved him so hard he fell over. He came up stunned and she was shouting at him.

"You stupid Touron! Are you trying to kill me?!"

"What?" gasped Billy getting to his feet.

"And what is this piece of crap kid board. It's not even a real surfboard!"

Billy was embarrassed and ashamed. He took his board and began to walk away.

It was Ted, Keaton's father, who saw the whole thing. He rushed out in the water and grabbed Jackie.

"Are you crazy or something?!" said Ted.

"But he dropped in on me. Twice!" she said.

Ted lowered his voice. "Go to the car Jackie."

"But Ted."

"I said go."

Keaton saw her father's mood and left with Jackie. Ted walked over to Billy, and he was as embarrassed by what Jackie had done as Billy was at being humiliated.

"I'm sorry fella. I really am. You okay?"

"Sure mister. It's okay."

You could cut the air with a knife on the way home. When Ted was really angry, he did not speak. The girls sulked into their seats.

"I am ashamed of you Jackie. That boy knew no better. Surfing is not about showing off. It's about loving the sea. And if you love the sea, you love everything about it. Even kids who don't know any better when they cut you off. You had an opportunity to make a friend. You could have explained what he was doing wrong, but you had to play the tough guy. Like you were superior to him. This is not what I taught you about surfing. About life for that matter."

Jackie started to cry a little. Ted had never said he was ashamed of her before. Because he never was. It was Ted who treated her like his own daughter and taught her to surf, who explained the codes and rules to her. It was Ted who went out of his way to bring her surfing when her parents could not. She loved Ted the way everyone loved him on the island. He had no enemies and was one of the best surfers on the Outer Banks. There was nothing worse to her than to know he was ashamed of her. She was his guest. It was just as bad as when her own parents were angry with her. Maybe worse.

She started to sob a little. "I'm sorry," she said. "I really am."

"So how can you fix this?"

"I'll tell him tomorrow if I see him. I promise. I'll tell him I am sorry."

Ted then smiled and Jackie saw it in the rear view mirror, as she was in the back seat.

"That's my girl," said Ted.

Jackie brightened up and sniffed.

"Ted," she said, "will you be mad long?"

"Naw," said Ted. And Jackie smiled.

The next day Keaton and Jackie walked over the dune as Billy and Timmy were strapping on the leash of their surfboards to their ankle. It was Billy that saw them first and sneered. "Here come the hot shots," he snarled.

Keaton and Jackie walked up to them and put the tail of their surfboards in the sand.

"I just want to say, I am sorry about yesterday."

Billy saw Ted standing off in the distance watching.

"Fine," replied Billy, "you put on a good show for your Dad. You can go now."

Jackie was upset. She really was a nice sensitive girl and hated she could not make things right. Not just for Ted, but for her. She had done a lousy thing and genuinely wanted to fix it. She waved Ted over.

"Oh great, is your Dad gonna push us around too?"

Ted walked over to the kids.

"This is Keaton's dad, Ted. I'm Jackie. And it's true, Ted wanted me to apologize. But I want you to know, and Ted, I'm apologizing because it was wrong what I did. And I am really sorry for it. And I would like you to forgive me."

Billy and Timmy could not believe it. Jackie's apology was all class: as was Jackie.

Billy smiled nicely. "Okay, it's okay."

"Good," said Jackie. "Now let me explain a couple of things to you so you won't mess up."

It was then that Jackie explained the unwritten rules of surfing to Billy and Timmy. They listened respectfully, wanting to fit in. Ted was proud of the girls once again. These were the girls he was raising.

All the kids then paddled out. The girls were the first out.

"Jeepers cats Jackie, how could you get mad at that cute boy?"

"They are cute, aren't they?"

"Duh," replied Keaton.

The boys struggled out and turned to get a wave. Billy stood right up in the white water.

"Look at that, Keaton. His second day and he's up. And look at his control and poise."

Timmy was next and also up.

"It took us a lot more time than that to stand up like that," said Jackie.

The boys were thrilled to stand up. But they were nowhere near as good as Keaton or Jackie. It was Jackie who explained how to stay in the curl and cut across the wave. Billy listened carefully. He tried it several times and fell. It was just too fast in the curl. But finally, it happened. A nice little three foot wave came right to him. He looked it over and noticed it was breaking to the right. He paddled in that direction, got up, and leaned to steer the board across the wave. The board responded and flew with blinding speed. It was all Billy could do to stay up, but he did. He rode the wave all the way to the beach.

"Go Billy!" yelled Jackie after him, although Billy did not hear her.

When he stepped off his board he was, different. He had never felt like that before. He had dreams he could fly from time to time, and this feeling was similar to the way he felt when he would awake form such a dream. He felt as if he had left the earth for a time. Like he was in another dimension. He looked at the board bobbing in the surf and picked it up with a sense of wonder. He pulled himself up on it and paddled out as the board planed over the water with a big smile on his face with his new friend, the surfboard.

"That was great. How'd you like it? asked Jackie.

"It was great. But, it's weird, I can't really describe it."

"I know," said Jackie, "that's surfing."

Everyday they met and rode the waves together as the hurricane built far away. After the fourth day Billy and Timmy were riding well. Billy was out in the surf and saw Jackie talking to Mr. Barnard. She was pointing to Billy and Timmy and then to her board. Mr. Barnard finally nodded and waved in Timmy and Billy.

"Jackie here thinks you guys are ready for some fiberglass boards, what do you think?"

Billy just about jumped out of his skin. He smiled at Jackie since he knew this was her doing. They all went to the surf shop together. Jackie helped Billy pick out a good board, not a real small one, but another eight footer since that would be in his league. It was, besides Jackie, the most beautiful thing he had ever seen. The rails, or sides, were white and the top was blue except for the middle, where a wide white stripe ran down the middle of the board. In the center of this stripe was another thin stripe which was called a stringer, a piece of wood to give the board strength.

"This is you," she smiled. "Yup, this will be perfect for you."

Keaton was busy picking out Timmy a similar board.

But strangely, right before they left, both Timmy and Billy walked over to the foam boards they had left off, who had shown them great things while keeping them from harms way. But as they stroked the boards for one last time, they felt good about leaving them. These boards were teachers, they enjoyed showing kids how to surf and then send them along. "We'll never forget you," whispered Timmy, feeling foolish, and Billy understood. "Let's go," said Billy.

And off they went to the beach with their boards strapped on their car. Mr. Barnard dropped them off at the beach.

"Now you be careful."

"We will," promised Billy.

They waxed up the boards like in the movies and were so excited they could barely stand it. When they finally had them waxed up and ready to go, they, all four of them, were facing the ocean where some nice two to three foot waves were coming in.

Jackie looked over at Billy.

"It was you who talked him into it," said Billy. "Thanks Jackie."

Jackie smiled big to him and said, "Okay Touron, you ready to ride or what?" and winked at him.

The boards seemed immediately to be in balance with Billy and Timmy as they paddled out. Keaton and Jackie had picked perfect boards for them. In no time at all they were riding the waves with their new boards. They were proud as they sat upon real surfboards. The sun was bright, the girls were prettier than ever, and Billy and Timmy were surfing now for sure. It was as good as it gets.

Billy paired off with Jackie and Timmy with Keaton. One evening the boys invited Keaton and Jackie over for dinner with their folks and they all had a great time. Keaton asked Ted if they could return the favor, and Billy and Timmy went to Ted's house to eat. His wife Karen was glad to have them. Out back they had a little soccer goal.

"You guys ever play?"

"Sure, we play."

Jackie was ready to show off with Keaton.

"How bout a little game, me and Keaton against you two."

"Sure," shrugged Billy.

Timmy and Billy went easy on Jackie and Keaton, let them score some points, and were impressed at how good they were. It was Timmy that was getting aggravated.

"I say we take the gloves off," he whispered to Billy.

"I don't know, they're girls."

"Cocky girls. We don't want to look like wimps!"

"All right, sure," said Billy.

Billy and Timmy came to the net, and as if they were not even paying attention, deftly maneuvered the ball around Jackie and Keaton to score three points in no time at all. There was nothing either of the girls could do to stop them. They could not outrun them, they could not steal the ball from them, they could not out think them.

"Now wait a darn minute!" screamed Jackie.

Everyone stopped playing.

"Who the heck are you guys anyway?" No boys have ever outplayed Jackie and Keaton like this before.

"You come out here and let us win and then beat the crap out of us. What's going on?"

Billy laughed. Finally, it was he who had something up on Jackie.

"He's captain of the team," said Timmy. "We won state last year."

"Jokes on us Jackie," said Keaton, "Looks like homeboys here got some game."

Jackie punched Billy in the arm.

"What the heck was that for?"

"For letting me win the first couple points."

Billy began to laugh with Jackie, and they went to have dinner next to the garden where a hummingbird flew to dine with them deep in the woods of Colington Harbor.

The storm was still brewing out in the Atlantic. The surf was building. Ted realized tomorrow would be the last day the girls could ride the swell. The day after would be way out of their league. But tomorrow would be the biggest surf they would have ridden so far.

Ted sized up the surf as they walked to the beach and decided they could still go out. Billy and Timmy joined them. The swells were generally about two to four feet with an occasional five foot set. There wasn't much of a rip and Ted knew all the kids to be excellent swimmers. They were all itching to get out there and try to ride the surf.

"All right," said Ted. "Let's go over some stuff. Rule number one?"

Keaton rolled her eyes; she had heard the rules before a million times.

"I said rule number one?" Ted said louder.

"Always know where your partner is," said Jackie.

"That's right. Keaton and Jackie, you are partners. Billy and Timmy, you're partners. Now never lose track of your partner. Never. Now, rule two."

"Know the depth of the water," said Keaton.

"So you don't break your stupid neck!" chimed in Jackie.

"That's right," said Ted. "But stay serious now. If it is shallow, you wipe out flat as you can so you don't bet banged up on the bottom of the ocean. And always protect your neck. Right?"

"Right," said Keaton and Jackie.

"I'm sorry, I can't hear you," said Ted

"RIGHT!" screamed all four kids.

"Rule three?"

"Keep the nose up!" said Keaton.

"And rule four?"

"If you wipe out, get away from the board. Don't get involved with rolling around in the surf with your board, unless you can't get away from it, then grab it and hold on tight so it can't bang into you. But best to get away from it if you can," said Keaton.

"And then what? What's the rest of the wipeout rule?"

"If you wipe out," said Keaton, "don't come up right away. Your board could be flying around in the air or who knows where. Let things settle down and come up with your hand and arm in front of your face just in case your board, or who knows what, is coming at you."

"And the most important rule?"

Jackie and Keaton laughed and shouted it together at Ted. "Never, ever, lose track of your partner."

"I'm sorry, I think I see four kids here."

At this all four kids: Billy, Timmy, Keaton, and Jackie screamed at the top of their lungs, "Never, never EVER, lose track of your partner!!!!!"

Ted was a little worried for them but did not show it although that little rule giving drama might have dropped a hint that he was a bit worried.

"Okay, go on."

They all stroked out together. The adrenaline was running high through the kids as they paddled high over the surf. Jackie was first to take off and got drilled. The wave was too fast for her. But she came up and paddled right out for another.

The next wave was Keaton's. She had better luck and positioned herself perfectly in the curl and flew past Jackie. This kind of pissed Jackie off. They never mentioned it, but there was a little subtle competition between the two of them. Ted was flying across one wave after another, as it did not seem big to him. Billy and Timmy were getting slaughtered, but kept coming back for more. Finally, they each caught a wave flew along with it.

Jackie was getting real pissed. She didn't seem to have any luck. The waves just were not coming her way. But then, there it was, and Jackie saw it first as her eyes grew round at the very sight of it. A rogue wave. Bigger than any wave so far; one of the first big swells from the hurricane. She scratched out far to go catch it. It seemed to grow exponentially the closer Jackie got. She put her head down and paddled with all her might. She looked up and and was for the first time in her life: scared. It had grown to six, seven, and finally eight feet and was already beginning to pitch. Jackie heaved and heaved for four more strokes, reeled around and tried to take a one stroke take off straight down the wave which was now practically vertical. No one could believe she was going for it, including Ted. She took off, tried to get up, but the wave was too fast, too steep. Her board went straight down toward the bottom of the sea taking her with it. The wave crashed over her and spun her around like she was in a washing machine. She remembered the first part of rule number four, the wipeout rule. On the way down she did everything she could to scamper away from the board; but she was losing air, began to panic, and forgot the rest of rule four: Let things settle down before you come up. Keep your hand in front of your face. But Jackie was a tad short on air and discombobulated from the wipe out: She popped up as soon as she could.

As she popped up, her surfleash snapped the board back at her while being pushed by another wave, whipping it right toward her face. What happened next was surreal. It was as if the board, instead of racing toward her, was traveling in slow motion. She knew she could not dodge out of the way, she could not get her hands up quickly enough to fend it off. It was as if she were in suspended animation and simply could not stop what was to happen next. Crack! The board slammed into her mouth and knocked her head back, stunning her. With blood filling her mouth, she tried to figure her next move. She looked out to the sea to see what was happening. And what was happening wasn't good. There was another wave, just as big as the first one, ready to crash down on her. Building power and strength, it smashed her to the bottom again. She had no time to dive to the bottom for safety. She took the full brunt of the impact. Down she went, weak and confused, with only a half breath of air, she tumbled around like a rag doll with the board and was hit again, this time breaking her nose. She fought to get away from it and finally did. The wave had passed and she weakly came up to the board, which was attached to her by her surf leash, to get air. She could barely hold on to it and began to slip off ;she fought hard to hold on; hard as she could she mustered up all the strength she had left over, and she just hung on to it weakly as the next wave took her down again. And this time she wasn't coming up.

When the wave came in that Jackie took off on, Keaton saw it, rolled off her board, and dove to the bottom for safety to let the wave pass over her, so she lost track of Jackie.

It was Billy who saw it all as he was paddling out. He pulled hard toward Jackie as he saw her weakly try to reach for her board and immediately alerted Ted. "Ted! Something's happened to Jackie!" he shouted. As he saw her try to hold on to her board, and then disappear underwater, his heart was in his mouth as he paddled toward her. "She's going down Ted!" he yelled. He paddled toward her scanning the surface of the water. "C'mon, c'mon Jackie. Come up come up," he was thinking. But he realized she wasn't coming up. "Ted!" he shouted once more, "She's not coming up!"

Keaton, Billy and Ted all stroked toward her. Ted, though he was much further from her than Billy, paddled like he and never paddled before and reached her first. He desperately looked around, saw her board, and knew she would be attached to it by her leash. He plunged into the water, grabbed her arm and rushed her to the surface. As he pulled her to the surface of the water he saw she was covered in blood and Ted gasped. But he was Ted and went into survival mode. The first thing to do was to see if she was conscious. "Jackie!" shouted Ted. "Jackie!" Ted screamed trying to get her back to her senses as he eyed another wave about to crash over them. "JACKIE!" boomed Ted right into her face, CAN YOU HEAR ME?!!!" Jackie then gave a small nod to Ted. It was all she had. "Listen! We're going down!" Ted saw the next wave rolling toward them, and the last thing he wanted was Jackie pummeled again. "Take a breath and hold it!" shouted Ted. As soon as Ted saw her inhale and close her mouth, he sucked in a huge gulp of air, put her in a cross chest carry, and pulled her toward the safety of the bottom. He then let the wave pass, and popped up. Jackie inhaled a huge breath of air. They were now out of the heavy impact zone. The white water was now easier to handle. Ted was horrified, but he would not let her know it. He reached to her ankle and snapped off her leash and pushed her up on his longboard in front of him. "C'mon cowboy," he said.

"Let's get out of here. Can you hang on?" Jackie weakly nodded, a wave came and they rode to shore. The kids were not far behind. Ted scooped Jackie up in his arms. As soon as Keaton saw the blood she started to cry.

"Keaton, Timmy, watch the boards. Billy, find the cleanest towel, shirt, whatever, white if possible, you can, shake it out, and dip in in the ocean and come with me."

Ted was going to need help, and Keaton was hysterical. Billy would stay focused. Ted would need the towel to put it in Jackie's mouth to try to stop the bleeding, which was tough since he wanted to apply pressure, but did not dislodge any possibly loose teeth. He thought he remembered salt water was good for that. He didn't have pure salt water, but he had the ocean, and hoped that was a good call. One tooth was already gone. Problem was, she was bleeding through her broken nose also. She was covered in blood, and he prayed it looked worse than it was since it was mixed with the salt water.

Keaton was in shock as she saw them run to the truck. She never cried, but she was crying now.

"She'll be okay, right?" she said to Timmy. "I mean she HAS to be. She's my best friend." Keaton could not help but to look at the sand with all the blood spilled all over it and remember Jackie's blood covered face.

"It'll be okay. Ted's got her," he said.

They both ran to the truck. Ted flew the doors open and handed Jackie to Billy. Ted saw she was rapped in the mouth, but what else was there he couldn't see? Did the board hit her in the head while she was rolling around with it? What was he dealing with? His mind raced for answers as to what to do. So he grappled for answers. He was angry answers eluded him and he was angry with himself for not knowing more first aid, but he did know quite a bit from boy scouts and lifeguarding. He had to act. He figured he has a missing tooth and maybe some loose ones with a lot of bleeding, the possibility of a head injury, maybe a neck injury, but probably not; she wiped out in deep water, but what if the force of the wave alone wrenched her neck? Probably not. He started making decisions fast. Try not to move her. Remember CAB, was that sill up to date?: circulation, airway, breathing, then immediately stop bleeding. Slow the bleeding down as much as possible, get her to the hospital. He once heard that if you had to do CPR on a person and they were bleeding, to immediately stop the bleeding after beginning CPR as a person can die rather quickly from loss of blood. Was that right? Didn't he hear that? Was it because the loss of blood would kill them as you gave them mouth to mouth? But that was probably a severe laceration or an artery hit, right? He told himself. This is just a busted mouth, *and a busted nose,* he regretfully added to that thought. That's a lot of busted stuff! How much blood could she afford to lose? The towel was soaking in it. Are there arteries in the face?

"How is she?" asked Ted.

Billy's voice shook as Jackie passed out. "Oh my God. She's out Ted. She's out."

"Shit!" said Ted through gnarled teeth and tried to think of what to do. If someone with a head injury goes out do you let them stay out as long as they are breathing, or do you force them awake. Ted couldn't remember.

"Listen good, real good," he said as he hit the gas. "Try not to move her from that position too much. Is she breathing? Put your ear by her mouth. Is her chest moving?"

"Yes, I think so."

Ted felt her wrist for a pulse and felt one. He put his hand on her chest and felt it rise and fall. "Thank God," said Ted.

"Okay. This is no time to lose it. Ya gotta help me." Ted was talking to Billy as a grown man and talking to himself as well. "Move her as little as possible, but don't let that blood drown her, you get me? Keep her head up, but a bit forward, with her head a bit forward: be careful the blood does not drain down her throat and choke her, apply some pressure to that mouth if you can, try to stop that bleeding too, but if there are loose teeth, don't loosen them up any more than you have to. And her nose, kind of pinch it off like this." Ted showed Billy how to pinch her nose to stop the bleeding, but make sure she's getting air through her mouth.

"Okay, I remember from first aid at school."

"Excellent! You pipe up if you think I make a bad call."

Billy did it. Jackie came around and the pain came again. She started to scream and cry and spit and cough up blood.

"It's okay, Jackie, I got ya," said Billy reassuringly. "Try not to move around too much."

But the pain was killing her.

Ted hit the gas hard. Should he have called 911 and waited for an ambulance? He once heard they had as much equipment as the ER. Did he hear that? But he already made the decision to go to the ER and had to stick with it right or wrong. The hospital was not far. Go! Go! he thought. He went through two red lights breaking the speed limit by twenty miles an hour. The limit was sixty. Ted was almost to eighty. A cop pulled out behind him and Ted made no motion to slow down. He screeched into the emergency ward, and laid on the horn. A nurse ran out to the car.

"I'm afraid to move her," said Ted. "It happened in the water. I don't know if there is a neck or head injury in addition to the smack on the mouth and the broken nose. Ted was happy to see the bleeding was slowing considerably thanks to Billy.

"She's lost a lot of blood," he said. Of course, that was obvious to the nurse as she saw the front seat of the truck.

"How long?"

"Ten, fifteen minutes. In and out of consciousness."

The nurse ran inside and out came three others who carefully placed her on a stretcher while stopping the blood and whisked her away.

She was then whirled away on a rolling bed to the operating room. Ted followed them and Billy stayed in the emergency waiting room. The cop ran up to the desk.

"What's wrong with Ted? I followed him over. What the hell's going on?"

The nurse explained what she could. The policeman went over to Billy. Billy began to sob and the cop pulled him over and gave him a hug. "It'll be all right. Don't you worry," said the policeman.

After an hour, Ted came out to see Billy.

"She's okay. Lost a lot of blood, and a tooth, but she'll be her old goofy self in no time."

Billy was so happy he almost cried. Ted patted him on the shoulder. "You did a great job Billy. A great job."

"Can I see her?"

"Tomorrow. She's resting now."

Billy looked as if he would crawl out of his skin.

"Okay, we'll just go for a look."

Ted and Billy slowly went to Jackie's bed where she was sleeping. Billy went over and stroked her hand.

"Okay?" asked Ted.

"Yes, thanks."

Ted then walked out of the hospital and went to pick up Billy and Keaton. They remained on the beach as he asked. They called no one on their phones in case Ted was to call them. They did not call

Ted so he could stay focused, and they wanted to be there when Ted returned.

He called them on the way and told them Jackie was okay. When he arrived, Keaton and Timmy ran up to him and gave him a hug. When they backed away, Ted took a long look at Billy and raised his hand for a high five. Billy smiled widely as they smacked their hands together triumphantly. Ted then grabbed Billy and gave him a very special hug. "You're the man, Billy. You're the man."

There was not a long time left in their vacation. One week. The doctors said Jackie could not surf for five days, and she sat on the beach every day and watched the others surf. Of course they all waited on her hand and foot. They went to the movies at night, played miniature golf, went for walks on the beach at night in front of the cottage. They told funny stories and laughed out loud at silly things.

One day Billy and Jackie were walking along the beach close to where her accident was looking for shells for Billy to bring back home. They were usual to Jackie, but they were unusual to Billy, who liked the flat pieces of shell with their different shades of blue and purple coloring. He found a few together and began to sift through the sand a bit to look around and felt something round, not like a shell. He sifted the sand a bit and rinsed the sand off it with the ocean water. His eyes grew wide as he stared at it. Jackie was a few feet behind him.

"Hey Jackie, look at this one." Jackie came up slowly as she was sure she had seen it a million times before. He opened his hand slowly.

"Oh my God!" said Jackie. She washed it off some more, and to be sure, pushed it in between the spaces of her teeth. A perfect fit. "That's it! That's my tooth!"

"From me to you Jackie. Bet you will always remember who gave it to you."

The next day Keaton was sitting on her surfboard looking at the ocean with Jackie at her side.

"I won't go out unless you come with me," she said.

The boys all agreed they would not either.

"Don't be ridonkulous. Go on," said Jackie.

No one moved.

"Go on!" yelled Jackie.

No one moved.

Jackie snatched up her board.

"Fine!" she said. "Maybe if I get my whole head knocked off, you will all be happy!"

She paddled out and they all followed her. They knew it was just a matter of time that Jackie would go back out.

A nice wave came right for her. She took a deep breath and paddled for it. But this time she rode the wave like Keaton. Gracefully, she cut across the wave, letting her hand run through the water. It was as if the ocean were apologizing for playing too rough. Jackie paddled out to the others smiling a smile that was missing one tooth.

She smacked her board and yelled at it.

"If you ever pull a stunt like that again, I promise you I will bust you in two across a telephone pole! And you," she slapped the ocean hard, "You!" Keaton, Jackie, and Billy were all stunned, what could she do to the ocean? Jackie's mind was racing for something to say. "And you!" she screamed, "I will crap on your stupid head if you do that to me again!"

Billy began laughing so hard he almost fell of his board. Keaton just shook her head toward Timmy.

"And as for you fools," grinned Jackie, "thanks."

That was all there was needed to say. All was back in sync now. The surfer girls were surfing again with their new friends, who would be leaving in two days.

Everybody was pretending not to be sad as Ted, Keaton, and Jackie were saying goodbye at Billy and Timmy's cottage. Ted and Mr. Barnard and his wife discreetly went into the house to give the kids a moment alone. It was the first time any of them had to say good bye to anyone they cared for that much. It was not like saying good bye to other friends or their grandparents who would be by again soon. This was a good bye that was special in a bad way. Because after their good byes the girls would never know if they would ever see Timmy and Billy again.

"It's for you," said Jackie as she handed Billy a little box.

Billy opened it, and there was Jackies' tooth, wound in silver wire dangling on a necklace.

Billy put it around his neck.

"It's the nicest present I ever got."

"From me to you," said Jackie and she began to cry, which surprised her but she could not stop it, and she felt stupid for doing so. "Bet you will always remember who gave it to you." And she paused and cried a little harder. "Right?" Jackie then tried to save herself from her emotions as she wiped away some tears. "You dufus Touron."

"I will," said Billy, and went to Jackie to hug her but she waved him off. "Not so fast," said Jackie, "I'm not done yet."

"But don't think too much about the bad parts," she went on, "like when I was mean to you when I first met you, and how I," and Jackie looked up at the sky as she said it, with tears still in her eyes, "never even properly thanked you for saving my stupid ass from practically bleeding to death."

She then looked over to Keaton. "And that's all KEATON'S fault!"

"My fault?!"

"Yes, YOUR fault! Why do you let me act like such a jackass? You should do something about it!"

Keaton, Billy and Timmy all started to laugh as Jackie regained her composure.

"So anyway, thank you," said Jackie.

"I won't forget anything about you Jackie. None of it I am sorry to say. Because I loved every minute of knowing you. Nothing, no one could make me forget you."

"Okay," sniffed Jackie, "then bring it in." She then opened her arms as a signal for a nice hug. Billy hugged her as if he would never let her go. But let her go, he must. He hugged her long and hard and then backed away and smiled at her. Jackie would never, ever forget that smile.

They all exchanged little presents. But none as nice as Jackie's tooth.

Billy and Timmy never felt so lonely as they watched Ted, Keaton, and Jackie disappear as they drove down the road. How could the happiest time they ever had in their life end this way, so sad, they thought.

Billy grasped his tooth in his hand and Timmy picked at a little bracelet Keaton had made him. Jackie had a tear well up in her eye as she held a ring labeled "State Champs" in her hand, and Keaton sighed as she held the silver necklace with half a charm Timmy had given her. Timmy reached down and thumbed the other half in his pocket.

Mr. Barnard put his hand over his wife's and she smiled toward him as their boys were growing up in the back seat.

Keaton and Jackie paddled out and waited for a wave.

"Did you ever kiss him?" asked Keaton.

"Right on the mouth!" said Jackie proudly.

"Me, too," smiled Keaton.

They then were sad in a wonderful way as they bobbed along in the ocean.

Sue was left in the pool of light bobbing around in the ocean with her friend. She was sad and happy all at once. She thought of being a young girl and the little romances she had when love was innocent and promised only kindness and devotion, and it warmed her heart to do so. She just lay back on the pillow and bathed in the innocence of this coming of age tale.

"Well?" asked Tom.

Sue said nothing and simply lay there.

"Well?" he said a bit louder.

Sue let him sweat for another minute, then she turned to him with a big smile on her face.

"Keeper!" she said.

She then looked over at Tom and asked, "Am I your surfer girl?" in a funny little voice.

"Do you surf?"

"*Do you surf?*" she mocked. She then straddled over him and put her hands on his shoulders and shook him. "I am ASKING if I am your surfer girl."

"But I never saw you surf . . ."

"Oh my frikkin gracious! Listen to me. You don't say, 'Do you surf?' you idiot. And as a matter of fact, yes I do. I just never surf around YOU cause I don't want to show you up. I surf all the big waves at Wiamea Bay and Pipeline and all over. I am the high royal princess of the waves for crying out loud. Now. AM I YOUR SURFER GIRL?!!!!"

"Yes, you damn liar, you are my surfer girl," Tom laughed as Sue shook him.

"Say it without the liar part!"

"But you are lying your ass off."

"You don't KNOW that. Now say it!"

Tom smiled a great smile. "You, Sue Coburn, are most certainly my surfer girl."

Then Sue got serious. "And we are going to have to part, like them," she said sadly as she slowly rolled off of Tom and along side him.

"Not like them, Sue, not like them," he said kindly, truthfully.

"Okay," said Sue. She then turned toward him, sleepy, and cradled toward him. "Cause I'm keeping my surfer boy." And they fell asleep as the moon yawned over a great sea path it lay over the ocean for dreamers to walk away from the continent and their problems to a fairy tale world over the horizon.

Chapter 14

The next day they went to the beach and the waves were small, but nice. Tom had his board under his arm and was eying over the break. Sue walked up.

"Give me the board."

"What?"

"The board, I want it, I want to, you know," and she jerked her thumb toward the ocean, "surf the waves."

"Don't be ridiculous. You could get hurt."

"*You could get hurt,*" she parroted

"You don't know what you're doing. This thing is hard and could smack you good."

"Give it," she said.

Sue just gave him a long look, Tom gave up, and he handed the board over. He knew there was no arguing with her and the waves were not very big. He would just keep a close look out for her. How hard could it be? she thought; you just paddle out there and stand up. She'll show him who his surfer girl is around here.

She snatched the board out of his arms and headed out to sea. She let the board glide over the first two waves. She liked the way it felt. Graceful and assuring.

She then slid on and began to paddle out. It was hard to get the center of the board beneath her and she struggled with it. Three waves knocked her off the board and she pulled it back with the leash. She finally got out beyond the waves and sat on the board and fell twice, then two more times. Frustrated, she somehow paddled in and threw the board onto the sand next to Tom.

"That freakin board is lopsided!" she hissed and marched to her towel.

Tom picked the board up and let her be, but could not help laughing under his breath.

"I can HEAR that Mr. Funny ho ho!" Sue yelled at Tom from her towel.

She was drying her hair with her towel and actually looked visibly upset.

"Hey, it took me a long time before I could stand up."

"Oh shut up," said Sue, and Tom did. He stood there saying nothing and Sue squinted up at him with the sun behind his head. "Oh, I'm sorry. It's just that, look at them," and she nodded to several girls on the beach with some boards. "The tight ass bitches are all over the place. Slip sliding around on the waves looking like some type of Greek goddesses or something. And then me. There's dufus me. And I'll be leaving. And they are all here."

"Those girls?" motioned Tom. "Why they're all whores and crackheads for crying out loud."

Sue chuckled. "They are not."

"Okay, they are not. You know what else they're not?"

"What?" sulked Sue.

"You," said Tom reassuringly.

Sue smiled up at him. "Wow. That was really good. That was the perfect thing to say. You are certainly improving. I could not have even thought of it."

"It's easy to tell the truth."

"There you go again! Unbelievable! Thank you," nodded Sue.

She then looked at the girls to the right of her who were waxing their boards. "And they are what?"

"Whores," smiled Tom.

"And you would never ever go out with them. Those nasty bitches. Right?" Sue said in a small way.

"Never ever," said Tom

He kneeled down next to Sue and kissed her.

"Freakin liar," she said.

Tom laughed and pulled Sue toward her. "Those girls have been here all summer. And I called you to come see me. Doesn't that count for anything?"

"Yes," she smiled. "I suppose it does."

"Hey, why not actually listen to me and let me teach you how to ride that lopsided board over there."

Sue looked at one of the surfers sliding gracefully across a wave. It did always mesmerize her.

"Wait a sec." She saw Tom scanning the beach.

He then walked to his backpack and walked over to a kid with a foam board and offered him five bucks.

"Here we go," said Tom pleased.

"Hey, you said I was going to ride THAT board," she said as she pointed to Tom's board.

"This is better for you."

Sue crossed her arms and tapped her foot menacingly.

"I don't want to ride it," she said.

"Why?"

She looked around and got close to his face so no one else could hear. "Because it's a WEENIE board," she snarled quietly.

"What are you talking about?"

"It's like the one in Surfer Girls. A weenie board. If I ride it, then I'm a weenie."

Tom laughed hard. "What are you afraid of? You won't look cool or something?"

"Yes, I am," she said sternly as she looked around.

"You're serious?"

Sue just stared him down.

"You'll look a lot less cool missing some teeth or crying cause you got hit on the noggin. C'mon Sue. You're a gorgeous girl. People will think you are cute on it.

"You think I'm gorgeous?"

"Even more so on this hot shot board."

"Allright," she said, "but I'm not giving in. I have decided it's a good idea all on my own. And I think I will look cute on it. Let's go."

Tom took her out and told her step by step what to do and was beside her the whole time. Finally after about a half an hour she caught one, managed to stand up and made it to the shore.

"Ha!" screamed Sue. "In your face bitches!" slipped out before she could stop it. Two girls who just arrived at the beach and were walking their boards out to the line up looked over at her. Sue was dying.

"I was thinking out loud, of these girls up north, who are just the worse! I'm sorry. I wasn't talking to you."

The two girls never really heard what Sue said, so they walked over to her out of politeness so they could understand her.

"I'm sorry, we couldn't hear you."

"That's good . . . I mean oh. I was just . . ." These were two young girls, and Sue stared at them with an inquisitive look on her face. She looked at them a long moment to the point where the girls got a little uncomfortable. It was the expression on her face, the way she was studying them. "You," said Sue, "you are . . . Keaton." Sue then slowly turned to the other girl. "And you. You're Jackie." She then looked up to the dune. "And there," she pointed, "that is your father . . . Ted."

The two girls stared at one another and then at Sue. "How did you know that?"

"I'm a witch!" exclaimed Sue, and the two girls jumped back a step. Sue began to laugh. She pointed to Tom paddling in. "He told me. I am visiting."

"Oh," said Keaton. "He and my dad surf together all the time. And he mentioned us?" Keaton and Jackie looked up at Sue and smiled as they wondered what Tom said about them.

"Yes, yes he surely did. He was *very* complimentary."

Keaton and Jackie began to giggle. Sue then looked at Tom, who was walking in, and out to the horizon and over to the dune in this now surrealistic day. She was now in a story, read beneath a lamp, behind a store in a fixed up room like an apartment. Tom walked in and said hello to Keaton and Jackie and eyed Sue over at the coincidence.

"Hey, you, you little surfer girls. I am new to this. And I think he is tired of me. Would you give me a few pointers? I would be most grateful," enquired Sue.

The girls were flattered this grown up, this very statuesque beautiful woman would ask for their help.

"Sure," said Keaton. "We'll help you. First of all, there are four rules you must know."

Sue took the board from Tom. "Excuse me, these two will take over now."

Sue spent the next hour laughing with Keaton and Jackie. She found out neither of them knew any boys from Arkansas and never were hurt surfing. But they yip yapped about Tom and Ted and boys in general. They immediately took to Sue and laughed and giggled away the day.

She had to leave the next day. There was no getting around it any longer. They lay together in the bed and Tom reached for a story. Sue snuggled in tight.

"Well, at least you are learning. I didn't even have to ask."

"This one is called Sans."

"After your sister."

"Yes. I used her name in it. I like to do that."

"That's nice. I remember her being very cute and funny. She is very nice, too."

"You remembered correctly."

Chapter 15

SANS

Sandra Johnson was driving down the Route 64 to the Outer Banks of North Carolina watching the trees pass by like hundreds of wooden soldiers. On each side of the road were drainage ditches that made mirror images of the forest. The forest was up in the air, and below the ground. It was beautiful to be sure, but not for Sandra.

"Stupid bastard," she spit through her teeth. Sean, her boyfriend of two years now, decides he wants to see other people. "Like what? Australian people? European people?" she joked. But it wasn't funny, he was referring to *female* people. It seemed when you graduated from college, couples either split up or planned engagements. Lucky her, her boyfriend decided to split up. That's just great. Thirty-five thousand dollars in debt for her education, not one bite on a decent job, and now she's dumped.

"Great day for me," she said happily with as much sarcasm as she could muster. She slumped down a little in the seat when her luck was about to get worse.

BLAM! The right rear tire blew! "Jesus!" cried Sandra as she grabbed the wheel and fought to control the car. Her mother, who listened to her husband, believed in hoping for the best and training for the worse. "The cost of safety is constant vigilance," Walt would say. So when Sandra was old enough to drive, she put her in the best driving school she could find. So Sandra's training took over as she was taught in class; she did not hit the brakes so as to not throw the car further off balance, and she reduced the speed of the accelerator slowly while trying to steer the car in the direction she wanted being careful not to jerk the car around to make matters worse until she could get to the shoulder. Her heart pounded as the car began to slow down and she heard the "whump, whump" of her flat tire and beating heart.

A wave of fear washed over her, left her drained, and then came the anger. "Damn it!" She pounded on the steering wheel and then the dash. "You son of a bitch!" she shouted at her car. "You and Sean and," she shouted out the window to the whole world, "and you too! You can all kiss my damn ass!"

She grabbed the wheel and started to cry. Her shoulders shook and she did nothing. "I give up," she whimpered. She sat all alone among the soldiers that could not help her and sobbed into her own loneliness.

"Here," he said. And without thinking she took a handkerchief from a gentleman who was standing by her window.

She did it without thinking and then the surprise hit her. She looked over and her eyes widened in surprise and she let out a little "Yah!"

He backed away. "Saw you at the side of the road and thought you may need some help."

She calmed, "Oh," and she smiled a little. "Sorry, you scared me. Having a bad day here."

"I can see that."

She looked up into his face. She, for some reason, did not feel suspicious of this man, here in the middle of nowhere, which was a better place than most to feel suspicious of someone; but she immediately felt comfortable with him. She looked in her rear view mirror and noticed he was driving an old Buick. He wore one of those hats that businessmen wore years ago. But his retro look seemed to fit.

"Just a flat," he said. "Where's the jack? We'll get you up and going in no time."

She noticed a strange familiar smell in the handkerchief.

"Let me have the keys, I'll get started."

But instead of going back to the trunk, he went back to his car and returned with a blanket and spread it on the ground next to the car.

"No use for both of us to get dirty. Have a seat."

For some reason nothing he did seemed odd to her. She wiped her eyes and sat down by the car as he began to change the tire. She began to feel good. Taken care of.

"You must think I'm an awful idiot crying over a stupid flat," she said.

"Blowouts can be awfully scary."

"Well, it's just been a lousy day for me. Stupid boyfriend dumped me. No job." She didn't know why she was telling him all this.

"Too bad to have a bad day on a gorgeous day like this. Just relax. Look around. Maybe things will get better."

She looked around. The birds were singing. It was fall and the temperature was perfect. Little humidity and about seventy-five degrees. The sky was cobalt blue and a breeze whispered through the trees, patted her cheek, and stroked her hair. And all of a sudden she was, happy?

She looked at the stranger who was about twenty-eight years old, and she felt this weird attachment to him. He was handsome, but something was all amiss. Who would wear those clothes today? Maybe he was headed toward Wilmington, a town in North Carolina that did movie shoots. But somehow he wore them comfortably to the point where he did not seem out of date.

The stranger lowered the car and put the jack into the trunk. She kept staring at him. He looked like an actor from an old black and white movie.

She could not stop herself. "Do . . . I know you from somewhere?" she asked.

He shut the trunk, turned, pushed his hat up on his forehead and gave a smile that stopped her heart. He then began to change right in front of her eyes. Into someone else.

"Yes, Sans, you know me."

A chill ran up her spine. It was not an actor from the past. It was a picture on the mantle.

"What the hell is going on?" she asked as she backed away. She was terrified, but the image she saw, she wanted to see. Her father was gone. Passed away when she was a little girl. This guy could be his twin.

"Who, who the hell are you? What the hell is going on?"

"You don't know me?"

"No, I don't know you."

"You can tell yourself that. Please don't Sans. Let go of your logic and good sense. Or use it if you like. You just saw a man morph into the image of your father. Why would I do that if I were not he?"

"I wouldn't know."

"When you were four, you were told never to get up on the chair to get to the cookie jar. You did it anyway and when you pulled it toward you it fell to the floor and broke. I saw you do it. It was a jar that was your mother's favorite, something that was given to her by her mother. I took the blame for it. Only you and I know that."

"How would you KNOW that?"

"You tell me."

"Daddy?" she said, as she squinted up looking into his face with her head cocked to one side. He stood still. She turned away, then back again and stared at him. Then finally, in inches and degrees, she realized the truth. It was him. Some part of her she did not really know or understand, but definitively believed, told her it to be so. She slowly, carefully, walked toward him, put her arms around him, and began to breathe deeply and calmly. She held him even closer and began to cry the happiest of tears.

"It's you," she said, "it's really you."

"It's me Sans," he said as he held her tight, the way he used to hold her as a little girl. Snug, just tight enough but not too tight. A hug that kept all bad things far away until they disappeared into space and kept all good things close at hand.

"So it's all true. You don't just pass away to nothing, like I feared."

"No. That's just you Sans."

"Wait, the flat, the car, The rumbling. Am I??? Is that it, I am . . . ? Her hand went to her mouth and her eyes grew round.

"Dead? No, no," he laughed. "You are quite alive as you know it. It was just a flat."

"What's it like?"

"Come here."

He then guided her past the trees by the road to a little pond. From the trees four deer appeared and approached them.

"Jesus!" she jumped as two large brown bears broke through the clearing.

"Don't worry," he said as they approached and he rubbed their ears.

Two foxes rubbed up against her leg and one jumped into her arms and she stroked its tail. Everything was peaceful here. And happy.

"They, *trust* us," she said.

"They trust me, and they trust you because you are with me. I come here often. I have seen you drive by lots of times."

"This is wonderful. I'll never worry about a thing again. Can I tell anyone?"

"You won't be able to."

"What does that mean?"

"You won't remember."

"Won't remember? How could I forget all *this*?"

"Well, you will remember, but not the way you think of as remembering. It's hard to explain."

Sandra began to cry. "And you are going to go? And I won't remember you?"

"Hold on Sans. Do you think this is the first time I have visited you, or your Mom?"

"You mean."

"And it won't be the last."

He leaned toward her cheek to kiss her good bye the way he used to when she was little.

"No, NO!" she screamed, "God almighty don't leave me!"

But before she knew what happened, he kissed her on the cheek and she was standing with this kind gentleman that was a stranger again to her. But she was, some kind of wonderful feeling: happy, content, blissful, secure, loved? What was it, she thought?

He led her to the car door and opened it for her and then closed it.

"You okay now?" he asked.

She looked at him in a daze. She felt so, bazaar, but nice.

"Yes, yes, I'm okay," she said as she stroked the steering wheel to her car. She loved this little car, she thought. "And, thanks, thanks for all your help. You really have been wonderful."

"Happy to help," he said. It was funny, she thought, he looked kind of sad.

She watched him walk to his car. She started her engine and pulled away. When she looked in the rear view mirror, his car was gone, which kind of shocked her. There were no side streets here. Must have turned around, she thought. But that was odd. She then saw his handkerchief on her seat and picked it up. She picked it up to dab at her makeup and a wonderful feeling filled her when she caught its scent. She pulled it away and looked at it in a peculiar way. She brought it up to her nose and again felt something strange and wonderful. She looked around and smiled.

"That Sean was a dick anyway," she said out loud and kind of laughed as she rediscovered herself. "I never liked him anyway. I'll get another Sean. A *better* Sean! That's what I'll do! Dufus! And his name won't be Sean either!"

She then laid the handkerchief on her lap, stroked it and drove home as she turned on the radio and was searching around for a station when something made her stop. She kind of cocked her head and listened for some reason. The song was Stardust. Her father's favorite song, she remembered. But it did not make her sad. She hummed to the tune as she remembered waltzing along atop her father's shoes as her face was pressed into his starched shirt. Without knowing it, she had the handkerchief up to her face as she breathed deeply.

She still has it and does not really quite know why. After all, it is a man's handkerchief. But she took it home and and washed it and happily placed it in her bureau drawer. But no matter how many times she washes it, it still has this wonderful aroma about it.

When she was a little girl, she used to cling to a blanket she called a "new," since when it was given to her it was new. It wore to tatters, and finally her mother and dad said they would fix it. They would take it to the blanket store and have them make it good as new, which was a bit ridiculous since there was only about a one foot long piece of it left that was two or three inches wide.

When they came back the blanket was full sized, the same color and texture. Sandra squealed with happiness and called this one her "new new." Pep and Walt Johnson gave a sigh of relief and laughed as they each picked her up and gave her a kiss. She was just the most cuddly of kids and loved to snuggle close. Sandra kissed Walt back on the cheek as she threw her arms around his neck and held to him tight, just as she did her new new.

She was remembering this all now for some reason as she put the handkerchief in her dresser drawer. She never gave it up. She still has it. If she ever goes somewhere, a job interview, a new city or town, a trip, she brings it along. It always comforts her for some reason.

Years later when visiting her mother, her mom unpacked her suitcase, saw it, and asked about it. Sandra was a little embarrassed and said, "That? That, is my new 'new new' if you must know."

Her mother looked at it strangely. She picked it up and gave it a long look. She then pulled it closer to her face and breathed in through her nose.

"You still have a "new new," she laughed, a very special loving laugh.

"Well, it's really a "new, new new," said Sandra feeling silly, "if you must know. Because, well, you know, there was the new, than the new new and, well, this one, this new new new. I guess you think I am just ridiculous." Sandra then looked around over both shoulders and whispered this biggest of secrets she told no one before. "But it's like, I don't know, it has this soothing power or something. Like my new and my new new. I know this is silly, but I can't part with it."

"Oh, I don't know," said her mother as she walked into her bedroom. "When I travel around I always bring something with me too."

She then handed Sandra a handkerchief exactly like the one Sandra had.

"I don't call it a new 'new new,' though, I call it Walt's handkerchief. Where did you get it?"

Sandra held her handkerchief next to its twin and gasped.

"From this nice man who helped me out one day," she said as she held both handkerchiefs ever so carefully. The memory was very odd to recall for Sandra. Part of her knew exactly what the man looked like and who he was, but another part of her didn't. She described him to her mother, but the description was nothing like her father. She thought this to be true as another part of her smiled and knew it was not. But there was no struggle between these memories: one cradled the other, as a father would cradle his little girl.

Sue was perplexed at the end of the story. Why? Why this story?

"Your dad just called the other day, right?"

"Yes, he's fine. It's just a story."

"And your sister, she is living in Jersey still?"

"No."

Don't you ask Sue Coburn, you nosy bitch. Don't you do it, she thought to herself, but it slipped out before her consciousness could stop it.

"So, where is she?"

"She moved."

"To where?"

"Why? What's the difference?"

"I mean, like Idaho or something?"

"She died. I think you have figured that out by now. Do I have to say it?

There, Sue had it. What the hell was the matter with her anyway, she thought. But she had to know for sure; why, she didn't know. Maybe so she could help him. Help this fellow swimming all alone far from shore who would not ask for help?

"I am a pushy, nosy, horse's ass, bitchy, lousy, gotta know everything awful person. I'm sorry I pushed it. I suck. I suck suck suck. SUCK."

"No, no you don't. If the shoe were of the other foot I may have done the same thing. And maybe it's good you pushed. I never talked about it to anyone, hardly. I just sucked it up. So here is a beginning. It was a terrible long death from cancer. The story, I guess, is assbackwards. Dad's here; she's there. And, I don't know, I mean, it is okay to be all cynical about religion and God when you are, well, until someone you love dearly dies. That's a game changer for sure. I just don't even know what to make of it all. It's just so everywhere and self encompassing." Tom lay back and said nothing. He then fought falling into the all too familiar void he tried so hard to stay away from.

"I'm all screwed up inside about so many big things," he said evenly, but a touch of sadness could not help being detected by Sue.

Sue waited. Tom put his arms under his head and stared toward the ceiling. Sue cuddled up to him and kissed him.

"I am here when you want to talk. But let me say this. You don't deserve this, or Sandra. It breaks my heart and makes my spirit rage to think the world can be so cruel."

"That's a piece of it." Tom felt a little better that maybe she did understand.

"I guess that was not a good pick, that story. It's kind of corny. But I kind of like it. I . . . I don't know . . . ," and he began to dangerously fall into the chasm that was blown into his life by this tragedy. He struggled not to. But he began to slip until something caught him.

It was Sue. She wrapped her arms around him and wouldn't let him fall, but in a way that if he did fall, she would fall with him and not let him get hurt. "It's a beautiful story," she said. "It's a fine pick. It is a wonderful story that throws some optimism on this frikkin rock we live on. I loved it. And you, you are a fine pick too, you cute rascal!"

Tom smiled. He let the fact that this beautiful girl next to him, who made him laugh and challenged him it the sweetest of ways, was here. And that his sister in his hope upon hope is okay. And why shouldn't she be? Would it not only make good logic that all will be fine in the end?

Chapter 16

They were at the airport, and Tom could go no further with Sue. He walked her all the way up to the point where only passengers could go on due to security. There was a line, and he walked with her until she had to show her ID and then put her possessions in a tray to be x-rayed. She looked up at Tom and had that look in her eye, and she was biting the nail of her little finger. She teared up a little. She looked around desperately. She needed something, something. Something.

"Give me your shirt," she said.

"What?"

"Your shirt, I want it."

"This is my favorite shirt."

"No, now it's MY favorite shirt."

"Oh c'mon Sue. Do you expect me to walk out of here half naked."

"I'll go on without it. And won't make a fuss, then." Sue began to walk toward the scanner not making a sound. It was the first time Tom saw her give up on anything. She walked quietly away and didn't look back.

"Hey," she heard Tom shout. She turned as he was taking off his shirt and threw it to her. She caught it with her smile and brightening eyes. She ran to Tom and hugged and kissed him. He hugged her back.

"Okay?" questioned Tom.

"No, just better," she said as tears welled up in her eyes. For Tom, for Sandra, for anyone who was ever alone and sad, and for these lovely, wonderful, seven days that relit her soul. "It's my new new," she said softly.

"I kind of figured," said Tom. He then smiled a smile he never smiled before. It was sad and happy and lovely. It was a special smile that may have never been seen if it were not for Sue. She was now two feet from him, the hug somehow broken and she could see this smile, this smile that she believed she understood, but she was Sue. She needed more.

"Say it or I won't make it," she said.

"It's your new new?" he said, perplexed.

"No, Duffus, the other thing. Stop it. C'mon, I'm *serious,*" she sniffled.

"Okay, just kiddin' around. I'm in love with you Sue."

"You're *in* love with me?"

"I am."

She grabbed his collar and looked him in the eye and said it, said it because it was surely true for now. And now was all she had at the moment. "And I'm in love you with you too. So, so very much," she said with all her fences down, moats bridged, and guards sent away.

She finally made it to the plane. As she got on, it was the same stewardess who called the cops on her. Sue was embarrassed and did not know what to do.

She kind of bent her head to the side and handed her the ticket as if she were someone else. When the stewardess looked up at Sue, she rolled her eyes, smiled, and said, "What are the odds?"

"Ohhh!" Sue stamped her foot a little at being identified.

"I am so sorry. But really, I am happy to see you. So I can apologize," said Sue.

"No need, your silly story is all over the airport. You are a bit of a celebrity." She looked down at the shirt. "His?"

"Yes, I snitched it off him at the gate," she said proudly.

Sue hugged the stewardess, and headed toward her seat.

That was the day that Sue flew away. Off the planet that held so many mysteries and stories and sadness and gladness. And Tom. Down there driving home. And she, she was leaving what she understood to be home, she thought. She scrunched the shirt up like a pillow and leaned on it by the window as she broke through the clouds. But things were different now. She had her new new to protect her, and a new life to live.

Thanks

Thanks to all the people I have met who's personalities I borrowed, and maybe tweaked, maybe didn't, to make this book. And thank you also to all the characters who introduced themselves to me through my imagination so I could write this book. Thanks Big Walt and Mom, Tom and Sandra. Thanks Ted. May we surf many more waves together.

And if you are reading this, thank you for reading my book. Say hello on my Facebook page, *Bedtime Stories from the Outer Banks.*